St27s

SHABANU

SHABANU

Daughter · of · the · Wind

BY

SUZANNE FISHER STAPLES

Alfred A. Knopf

New York

THIS IS A BORZOI BOOK
PUBLISHED BY ALFRED A. KNOPF, INC.

2   4   6   8   0   9   7   5   3

Library of Congress Cataloging-in-Publication Data
Staples, Suzanne Fisher.
Shabanu, daughter of the wind / Suzanne Fisher Staples.
p.   cm. Summary: When eleven-year-old Shabanu, the
daughter of a nomad in the Cholistan Desert of present-
day Pakistan, is pledged in marriage to an older man
whose money will bring prestige to the family, she must
either accept the decision, as is the custom,
or risk the consequences of defying her father's wishes.
ISBN 0-394-84815-2 ISBN 0-394-94815-7 (lib. bdg.)
[1. Cholistan Desert (Pakistan)—Fiction.
2. Pakistan—Fiction. 3. Sex role—Fiction] I. Title.
PZ7.S79346Sh   1989   [Fic]—dc19   89-2714

To the people of Cholistan

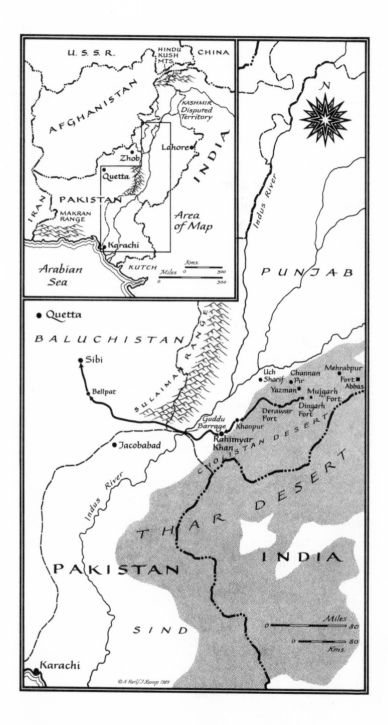

Names of Characters

italicized syllable is accented

Shabanu (Shah-*bah*-noo)—Narrator, eleven years old at the story's beginning

Phulan (*Poo*-lahn)—Shabanu's sister, age thirteen

Mama (*Mah*-muh)—Shabanu's mother

Dadi (*Dah*-dee)—Shabanu's father

Dalil Abassi (Dah-*lihl* Uh-*bah*-see)—Dadi's proper name

Jindwadda Ali Abassi (Jihnd-*wah*-duh *Ah*-lee Uh-*bah*-see)—Dadi's father

Adil (Uh-*dihl*)—A married male cousin

Hamir (*Huh*-mihr)—The cousin to whom Phulan has been promised in marriage

Murad (Moo-*rahd*)—Hamir's brother, whom Shabanu will marry when she comes of age

Sardar Nothani Bugti (Sar-*dahr* Nuht-*hah*-ni *Buhg*-tee)—Leader of a clan from the Bugti tribe of Baluchistan

Wardak (*Wohr*-duhk)—An Afghan rebel leader

Sharma (*Shahr*-muh)—A female cousin of Dadi's

Fatima (Fah-*tee*-muh)—Sharma's daughter

Nawab of Bahawalpur (Nuh-*wahb* of Buh-*hah*-wuhl-poor)—The hereditary ruler of the old kingdom of Bahawalpur, now a district of modern Pakistan

Sulaiman (Soo-*leh*-mahn)—Keeper of the tombs at Derawar

Shahzada (Shah-*zah*-duh)—The guard at Derawar Fort

Bibi Lal (*Bee*-bee Lahl)—Murad and Hamir's mother

Sakina (Sah-*kee*-nuh)—Bibi Lal's youngest daughter
Kulsum (*Kool*-suhm)—The widow of Lal Khan, Murad and
        Hamir's older brother
Nazir Mohammad (*Nuh*-zeer Muh-*hah*-muhd)—A
        landowner at the village of Mehrabpur
Rahim (Ruh-*heem*)—Nazir Mohammad's older brother
Spin Gul (Spihn *Gool*)—An officer of the Desert Rangers
Colonel Haq (Colonel *Huhq*)—The commander of the
        Desert Rangers' headquarters at Yazman

SHABANU

Guluband

Phulan and I step gingerly through the prickly gray camel thorn, each of us balancing a red clay pot half filled with water on our heads. It was all the water we could get from the *toba*, the basin that is our main water supply.

Our underground mud cisterns are infested with worms. We'll dig new ones when the monsoon rains come—if they come.

The winter sky is hazed with dust. There has been no

rain in nearly two years, and the heat of the Cholistan Desert is as wicked as if it were summer.

Phulan walks with her eyes down, her feet shuffling, kicking up puffs of sand that is light as dust. Her name means "flower," and she is beautiful when she smiles.

I am Shabanu. Mama says it's the name of a princess, but my red wool shawl has worn so thin I can see through it. I pull it tighter around me and pretend it's a *shatoosh*. It's said that real princesses wear *shatoosh* shawls so fine they can pass through a lady's ring.

In the courtyard that circles our round, thatched huts, Mama and Auntie have made a fire, and a kettle keeps warm beside it for tea. Even when we are down to the last of our water we have tea. Grandfather leans against the courtyard wall, chin on his chest, his turban nodding in rhythm to his snores.

Mama sits with yards of yellow silk in her lap, stitching one of Phulan's wedding dresses. She has embroidered silver and gold threads, mirrors, and tassels into the bodice. You'd think Phulan was the princess!

Mama holds up the tunic and measures it against Phulan's shoulders and chest. She laughs, her teeth gleaming in the opal haze of the setting sun.

"If you don't grow breasts soon, this will look like an empty goatskin," she says, her strong brown fingers plucking at the extra silk in the curved bodice. She has made it big enough to fit Phulan when she's grown. Phulan is thirteen. She will marry our cousin Hamir this summer during the monsoon rains. The monsoon, God willing, will bring food for our animals and fruit to the womb of Phulan.

"If God had blessed you with sons, we wouldn't have to break our fingers over wedding dresses," says Auntie as she sews the hem of the skirt. Her sons, ages three and five, play noisily nearby.

Mama ignores her and sets the silk aside, for Dadi will come soon from tending the camels, and he'll be hungry. She dips her tall, graceful frame through the doorway of our hut and comes out with a large wooden bowl. Squatting before the fire, she kneads water into wheat flour to make *chapatis*.

"I worry," Auntie goes on, her fingers flying over the yellow silk. "You'll spend your life's savings on two dowries and two weddings. Without a son, who will bring a dowry for you? And who will take care of you when you're old?"

Mama pulls at the dough and slaps it into disks. She whirls the flat bread onto the black pan over the fire.

"Mama and Dadi are happy," I say, sticking my chin out.

"What do you know?" Auntie asks, folding her pudgy arms over her bosom. "You're nothing but a twig."

"They laugh and sing. Aren't you happy, Mama?" Mama smiles, and her eyes are merry in the glow of the fire. Auntie almost never laughs.

"Don't worry, little one," says Mama. "You and Phulan are better than seven sons." Auntie purses her lips and picks up her sewing again.

Phulan covers her nose and mouth with her shawl, and her eyes tell me she is trying to keep from laughing. Auntie gives us a sour look and bends over her work.

Dadi and I bought the silk—meters and meters of red and turquoise and yellow the color of mustard blooms—on our way from the great fair at Sibi last year.

Dadi comes into the circle of the fire as the light is leaving the sky and the stars begin to peep out from their sapphire curtain. He is no taller than Mama, but his shoulders are broad and the *lungi* tied around his waist covers the thick muscles of his thighs and buttocks.

"How much water is there?" he asks, crossing his ankles and sitting beside the fire. He rubs his eyes. They are red, irritated by blowing sand. Most of the desert plants have died from lack of rain.

Phulan fetches Dadi's *hookah* and lights it with a stick from the fire. Dadi sucks on the snakelike mouthpiece, and the sweet smoke of brown sugar and tobacco bubbles through the water in the base of the long pipe.

Mama looks up at him from across the fire.

"We have two goatskins, one half full. One pot is empty."

Phulan's eyes are intent on Dadi. He has just come from the *toba,* where the camels gather each day to drink.

"What's left in the *toba* is not fit for the camels, let alone for us. We must pack tomorrow."

We are the people of the wind. When hot summer winds parch the land, we must move to desert settlements where the wells hold sweet water. When the monsoon winds bring rain, we return to the dunes. But this year and last the monsoons failed, and we must go now to Dingarh, an ancient village where the wells are deep.

"You'll take me away, and I'll never come back to Cholistan," Phulan says softly, looking at her hands.

"Nay, nay," says Mama, leaving her *chapati* making to pull Phulan into her arms. "We'll settle at Dingarh before Dadi and Shabanu leave for Sibi next month." Mama rocks Phulan against her. Dadi says nothing. His face is tired from worry, and his black hair is disheveled under his turban.

I secretly count the hours until we leave for Sibi! It will be just Dadi and me and the camels. Phulan hasn't gone since her betrothal to Hamir. Our camels are always the finest at the fair, and Dadi is a good businessman. This year we'll sell fifteen to pay for Phulan's wedding.

The winter night is cold after the intense heat of the day, and Phulan and I huddle under the quilt for warmth. There is scarcely any space between the stars. I watch them as Phulan talks about having babies. No matter how I try, I can't imagine her a mother. But her monthly bleeding began, and Mama and Dadi quickly set her wedding date for the summer, after the fasting month of Ramadan.

"You'll have new clothes too," she says, hugging me close. I've worn the same tunic over the same skirt three years, since my eighth birthday. They used to be blue as the winter sky, with red flowers and ribbons. But now they have no color at all. The buttons are gone, the sleeves are up to my elbows, and the skirt is nearly at my knees.

"How I'll miss you next winter!" I say. "It will be so cold without you under the quilt." I regret the words the second they're out. Phulan's moods are fragile.

"I'd rather die than leave the desert," Phulan says, her whisper shaking in my ear.

"Of course you wouldn't," I scold. "You'll have babies of your own, and I'll be with you next year." I brush her tears away.

But I am frightened too. Next year I will be betrothed to Murad, who is Hamir's brother. The people among whom they have settled in the irrigated area call us gypsies and accuse us of stealing their animals and food. Last year we went to Mehrabpur for Mama and Dadi to discuss the marriage with Hamir's mother. Our dog was poisoned. Someone stole a baby camel.

This year we will go to Mehrabpur for Phulan's wedding. Next year we will go back for my wedding to Murad, and each year thereafter when the *toba* is dry Mama and Dadi will go there to graze the animals and visit us. Mama says it's a good match, because Hamir and Murad have land. Dadi will give us each ten camels with our dowries.

"Don't worry," I say, smoothing Phulan's hair and kissing her tears. But both of us know that their ways are strange, and there are unimaginable things to cry about. Phulan cries herself to sleep.

I awake in the morning, shivering like a baby camel. The sky is gray with tumbling clouds. I crawl out from under the quilt, and the rain begins with large splatters of water that send little puffs of dust up from the ground.

Dadi is outside the courtyard unloading the camels. He and Mama have been up before daylight packing wheat and milk, bedding, and our belongings onto the animals' backs. Mama dashes back and forth across the courtyard pulling saddles and blankets into the house again.

"Wake up, Shabanu!" she says, her voice bubbling. She and Dadi have prayed hard for rain, a rare blessing in winter. "Don't stand there like a stump! Can't you see its raining?"

"Phulan!" I shout. "We can stay!" She darts out of the house like a sparrow. We hug each other and dance up and down.

"Watch out, you'll knock over the milk pots!" says Mama, but she is laughing too.

We spend all day inside our round mud house, birds chirping in the snug thatched roof. Dadi brings us camel harnesses to mend, and Grandfather tells stories about his days as a great warrior in the Army Camel Corps of the Nawab of Bahawalpur. His thin, wrinkled face is animated, his eyes lively. Usually he is half-asleep, and we are happy to hear his voice, rough as the windblown sand, telling stories of defending the desert against the Rajput princes from India.

The rain makes us giddy with its bitter, fresh smell. We keep a fire going all day, boiling milk, making tea, and celebrating the rain, not minding the cold.

The rain beats down all morning, but we are safe and dry under the thatch. Sharp bluish smoke from the fire rises in a slow, twisting ribbon and escapes magically through the branches that keep the rain out. By afternoon it's raining so hard we can barely hear the thunder, and Dadi builds a doorsill of sticks to keep the water from pouring in.

Toward evening he announces he will go out to the *toba* to see how much rain has collected.

"Are you mad?" asks Mama. "There is no such thing as too much water! The *toba* will be there in the morning, and the fuller the better."

Dadi sighs and sits down again. But he is happy.

While Mama fixes *chapati*s and spiced lentils for our dinner, he sings a desert poem, his voice husky and clear like wood smoke.

Auntie says little, except to cluck at her boys who have grown restless indoors all day.

Auntie is married to Dadi's brother. Uncle lives in Rahimyar Khan, where he works in a government office. Uncle comes several times a year, bringing Auntie gifts—quilts, shawls, and brass pots. He brings us vegetables, wheat, and lentils. Auntie is lonely. She feels superior to us because of Uncle's salary and her two sons. But she does her share of the work and is kind to Mama.

It rains all night, and in the morning Phulan and I crawl out from under our quilt, teeth chattering. Mama hands us each a cup of milk tea.

The air is clear—I can smell the sweet absence of dust.

The sand sparkles like water, though the early morning breeze has dried it to powder again. Tiny purple flowers cover the ground, where two days ago there was nothing but camel thorn. The winter sky is blue-green above the lavender line that rims the horizon.

Across the courtyard Auntie comes out of her hut, tucking quilted jackets under the boys' round chins. She pulls them close to the fire.

"Did God give you rest?" she asks. Mama greets her back.

The sun spreads an orange wash across the swept mud floor, and mellow points of light glint from Mama's silver bracelets. I am impatient to take Guluband to the *toba* to see how much rain has collected. I take the goatskin and water pots to where he stands tethered to a wooden stake at the edge of the courtyard.

"Phulan, stop daydreaming and bring more milk," says Mama. Phulan opens the rough wooden door to a baked mud mound at the edge of the courtyard, where the camels' milk will keep cool through the day. She reaches inside and pulls out a round earthen pot. I rub Guluband's nose and slip a piece of brown sugar under his lip. He grunts softly as I take his reins.

"Uushshshsh," I say softly. "Uuuushshshshshshsh." He dips his great head, roaring a protest as he always does, perhaps to let the world know he is a camel. He folds his front legs under him and kneels, sinking quietly to the ground. I fling the goatskin over his shoulder and attach the earthen water pots to his wooden saddle. I climb up behind his hump and twine my fingers into curls of rough brown hair to hold my seat while he lurches to his feet.

Guluband lifts his head and we survey the gray desert, rising and falling like the Arabian Sea beyond the dunes, with misty mounds of *pogh* and thorn trees floating for hundreds of miles around. I squint and look at the dunes on the horizon, which is inside India.

Sometimes our animals wander across the border, and when I go to fetch them I look hard to see how it differs from our Pakistan. But the same dunes roll on into India, and I can't tell for certain exactly where Pakistan ends and India begins.

Without a signal from me, Guluband turns toward the *toba,* his feet whispering in the powdery sand, his powerful legs unfolding and stretching in a loping rhythm as ancient as the desert. I think of leaving Cholistan, and my chest swells with a pain so deep it closes my throat and sends tears to my eyes.

"Guluband, *ooh chumroo, tori totoo, mithoo* Guluband," I sing to him softly. His furry ears swivel backward and his feet pick up the rhythm of my voice, the brass bracelets around his legs jangling. His knees lift against his chest, his back legs striding twice for every step of a foreleg. His neck absorbs the rhythm, his head high and steady, and I feel there is nowhere else so grand on earth.

Dadi earns extra money taking Guluband to dance at the fairs in the irrigated areas. When my cousin Adil was married last year, Guluband danced for hours. Usually it takes drums and pipes to put him into the mood. But I can make him dance with just a song.

We round the last stand of desert shrub and Guluband drops his head, his nimble lips plucking at the thorny stems. His mouth is tough as rhinoceros hide. We are just at the base of the last sand dune before the *toba*, and I hear Dadi singing and shouting on the other side. It must be full of water!

I cluck at Guluband and tug gently on his reins. He knows me well enough to sense I'm in a hurry, and his great legs stretch out, lifting us up and over the dune.

"*Allah-o-Akbar!*" shouts Dadi, his head thrown back and the veins in his neck sticking out like goathair cords. He is knee-deep in the *toba*, and his turban falls into the water. His *lungi* also hangs in the water, absorbing it like a thirsty wick. "God is great!" he sings out again, and begins to laugh.

When he sees me, he grabs up his turban and *lungi* and gallops through the water, across to me on the other side. He reaches up to haul me off Guluband's back. Again he throws back his head.

"*Allah-o-Akbar!*" He tosses me into the air, catching me in his strong, lean arms. The water stretches for miles around us, and the camels that have gathered at the edge to drink look at us as if we are mad. Even the females who haven't had their babies return from the brush to drink.

11

"How long will the water last?" I ask, not daring to hope it will be enough to stretch through until the monsoon rains in July.

"We can stay perhaps until Phulan's wedding," says Dadi, his smile dazzling under his thick black mustache. I throw my arms around his neck and hang on, happy as I ever remember being.

He lifts the water pots down from the saddle, and Guluband lowers his head to quench his thirst. Although the herd has been at the *toba* most of the night, many camels still stretch their necks to drink.

I wade out into the clear water to fill the goatskin bucket. It's icy, but I'm too happy to care. I return to the edge and fill two pots from the skin. Dadi lifts one to my head and waits for the sloshing load to settle before setting the second atop it. I stand motionless beneath their weight while he fills two others.

They shine when he fastens them to the saddle as though God had sprinkled them with diamonds.

Birth

I see the vultures just before noon—a lazy, circling reminder that life is fragile. Normally snakes and scorpions spend the cold weather underground. But rain in January fills their holes and tunnels, forcing them out, angry and confused, and they bite anything that moves. So the vultures make long, lazy loops in the sky, prowling for anything that falls.

It's my turn to tend the herd and I am busy. After a

rain the camels don't need to stay near the *toba*—water is everywhere, and they wander where they want. When the weather is dry, the *toba* is like a magnet; eventually they all come back to drink.

I notice the circle of birds tighten and then hear a dreadful bellow. I am running, my heart on fire, before the first yellow bird dives. The birds gather behind a spiky clump of *pogh,* dropping from the sky now like heavy, feathered sacks. The yellow-gray wings flap furiously. The bellowing continues, though weaker now, and I know the camel is still alive. My legs carry me with what seems like superhuman speed; still it's forever before I reach the dying female.

I wade in among the swarming mass of feathers, shrieking animal warning sounds, waving my arms and beating at the great bald-necked vultures that have gathered at the camel's head, waiting to feast greedily the second life leaves her.

More birds, each nearly my height and weight, hover around her hindquarters, waiting to disembowel her. Or so I think until I move around for a full view.

The birds are after her unborn baby! Only its head and front feet extend from the mother. The sack has burst, and the baby's eyes are shut tight against the brilliant sun. It isn't breathing yet, but the mother has lost the strength to push, and I know if I can't pull it out, it will die.

I am exhausted from running and chasing away the vultures. I can't think what to do. I take another look at the mother's face. She has stopped struggling, and her breath comes in short gasps. Her legs are rigid in front of her. Bending closer, I see the swollen flesh around two puncture marks on her nose. I think she's been bitten by a krait, a snake even deadlier than the cobra.

Camels give birth lying down, but the second the baby is born the mother stands, and the baby tumbles out onto the ground. The shock breaks the cord and knocks air into the baby's lungs. This mother will be paralyzed within minutes, and unless I can birth the baby, it will die.

I grab the baby's head and pull, but there is no give. I pull gently at first, then in desperation I begin a steady pressure with all my strength, one hand behind the baby's head, the other gripping his forelegs. I stop to rest, panting, tears streaming down my face, and notice an inch of neck, wet with mucus, has been born.

With a grunt, I grab both forelegs now and give a mighty yank. Nothing happens. A memory takes shape in my mind of fetching boiled water to a room with moans and soft cries slipping like ghosts through the shuttered windows, of Mama lying across Auntie's heaving stomach, a woman from the village pulling at something between Auntie's splayed, bent legs.

I run to the mother camel's side, screeching at a vulture perched there. She still pants softly. I throw myself across her swollen belly and grab her spine, pressing myself against her with all my might. There is a small gasp, and I slip off, grabbing the baby's forelegs again, hauling with all my might. An inch of wet shoulder appears. My dress is soaked with sweat from the effort, and I wonder if the inert baby has been poisoned too and whether if he survives the birth he will find a foster mother. In the January sunshine of a day that began with happiness, suddenly death seems easier, more inevitable than life.

I think of Phulan giving birth, still a girl, in a strange bed with a woman she barely knows yanking at a half-born child between her legs. I hear a low wail and realize it is coming from me.

I take the baby camel's face between my hands and his nostrils twitch. Again I grab his forelegs with strength that I believe now comes from God—surely I have none left myself. The baby's chest is out now. Again I fling myself across the mother's belly. She grunts and I know she is still alive, though the vultures stand now on her neck. I scream at them and they flutter lazily.

I haul on his legs, and the baby is half born. I pray for the mother to go on breathing, to keep the baby alive until I can pull him into the world and he can breathe for himself.

I don't know how long it takes, but by the time his back legs are free he is bleating and wriggling, trying to stand. I bite the cord, freeing him forever from his dying mother. When that is done, I turn and look at her. "Your baby is safe," I say. A vulture standing on her forehead ducks its head, and its hooked beak pierces her lifeless eye.

I beat at the vultures again, but they are already tearing at the carcass of the dead mother. I clean the baby with my shawl, trying to ignore the gurgling sounds and the flapping wings behind me. I rub his legs and chest briskly until his soft white fur curls tightly as it dries in the sun. Slowly he becomes more active. All the while he nuzzles me, looking for a teat to suckle.

My legs tremble, and I feel ill. As soon as the baby is able to organize his long, trembly legs, I take my scarf from my neck and tie it around his and lead him slowly away, back to the rest of the herd.

At the *toba,* it seems impossible that life is going on as if this had never happened.

We have six new babies in our herd, all healthy and nursing. I take the new one to the other mothers, but they lower their heads and trot away. He follows me closely, as if I am his mother. But I can't feed him, and he'll die if I can't find a nursing female for him.

Under a thorn tree are two of the water pots Dadi and I filled in the morning. Suddenly I am thirsty and too tired to move. The baby and I rest under the tree, and I lift a pot to fill my cup. The baby smells the water and nudges me, gently at first. I dip my fingers into the cup and hold them out to him. He sniffs gingerly, then sucks greedily, grunting. With difficulty I free my fingers to wet them again. Lying under the thorn tree, I feed him until we fall into exhausted sleep.

When we awaken the sun is lower, and the sky has turned to opal, inevitable dust creeping into the air. In the distance I hear the *kachinnik, kachinnik, kachinnik* of Guluband's leg bracelets.

"Ho! What's this?" Dadi shouts, climbing down before

Guluband can kneel. He runs to us. Phulan is covered head to foot in a *chadr*. Now that she is betrothed, she can't leave the house without the billowy veil—and she still can't get down from a camel gracefully while keeping herself covered.

I'm so relieved to see them that the words spill out of my mouth in a jumble, and before I can stop them, tears are streaming down my face again. Dadi listens, inspecting the baby's mouth, ears, feet, and eyes. I choke to keep from sobbing, and he turns to look at me. His eyes are half angry, half hurt.

"Take me to see," he says.

For a moment I stare at him, then I understand that this baby and his mother were to be part of Phulan's dowry.

I stroke the baby's tiny ears and wobbly head. "I think it was a snake bite." I point in the direction of the flapping swarm of vultures. Dadi goes to have a look.

Phulan sits on the ground, wraps her *chadr* tightly around her knees, adjusts it over her face, and huddles into its folds. She's so pleased with herself. We are good Muslims, but God doesn't care what color *chadr* she wears. She has chosen black, and wears it like a martyr.

"You don't have to hide from me," I say, and we're both surprised at the anger in my voice. She lets go of her knees and leans over to push my hair from my face. I can't stop the tears again.

Dadi returns.

"You did well to save the baby," he says, and sits down beside us.

"None of the other mothers will nurse him," I say. "But he'll drink water from my fingers."

"You'll work full time to feed him that way," Dadi says.

Phulan picks up her milk pot and heads toward a female with a yearling that's nearly weaned. A woven bag is tied over her udder. We use most of her milk ourselves. With hope in our hearts, the baby and I follow Phulan. But she shoos us away. We go back and wait under the tree.

The baby bleats softly. I know he's hungry. I untie a cloth wrapped around the *chapatis* from lunch, but the baby isn't interested. The sun is sinking and the air is cooler, the shadows growing longer and less dark.

When Phulan returns, I fill my cup with milk. The baby smells it and stumbles in a hurry to stick his nose under my arm. I dip my fingers into the warm, salty milk, and he nearly knocks the cup from my hand as he grabs at my fingers. Dadi is right. I can't feed him enough this way.

I raise my arm so my fingers point downward, like a mother's teat, and the baby tips his head back to nurse. Slowly Phulan pours milk down the back of my hand so it runs down my fingers into his mouth. His tail flicks, and for the first time today I think he'll survive.

Kalu

I name the baby camel Mithoo for the sweetness of his nature. He's grown enormous in a month, all white curly fur, big round feet, his head as high as my own. He follows me everywhere, nibbling at my hair and pulling at my sleeve.

The days are warmer now. The air is still clear, and the nights are cool. Flies buzz lazily as I sit in the shade of a thorn tree watching the herd, picking ticks from Mithoo's legs and daydreaming about the Sibi Fair.

Mithoo lifts his lip in a toothless smile—he won't have milk teeth for another month—then gallops off, legs flying for joy until they tangle and he lands like a pile of sticks.

Dadi and I leave for Sibi soon. Mama made me a new long skirt and dress for my twelfth birthday. They're the first grown-up clothes I've ever owned. The skirt is blue, dark as the night sky, with pink blossoms, embroidered with tiny mirrors that sparkle at the hem. I'll wear it when we set off. I don't know when Mama found the time, with gathering wood and helping Dadi and making Phulan's clothes and mending the mud walls and cooking and repairing the quilts.

I turn at the sound of Guluband's bracelets. It's Phulan, wrapped inside her black *chadr,* bringing me *chapati*s and milk tea. She's in her own world these days, caught up in plans for the wedding, wanting to know everything about Hamir and his family, and totally uninterested in her chores.

There has been no more crying under the quilt. As Muslim girls, we are brought up knowing our childhood homes are temporary. Our real homes are the ones we go to when we marry. I wonder how I can ever accept a place outside the desert, without my camels and Mama and Dadi.

Phulan gets down from Guluband's back without tripping over her *chadr.* Mithoo runs over to see if she has anything for him. She sticks a long slender hand out from under her black wrapping and offers him a lump of cheese.

We laugh at the face he makes at his first taste of hardened sour curds.

A loud bellow interrupts us and we turn to watch Tipu, the stud of our herd, court a female he fancies. He gallops along the edge of the *toba,* a large pink bladder gurgling from the side of his mouth. Perhaps God knows why this is attractive to a female camel, but his target, a young female in her first heat, lifts her head and answers him with a loud bleat.

Tipu mates three or four times a day. His belly is high and tight, the muscles along his back and haunches bulge from his strenuous mating activity.

He trots up to the female, his teeth squeaking as they grind together. A rumbling starts deep in his belly, emerging through the pink bladder in a slobbering, foamy belch. Tipu shakes his head, and the foam flicks out, sticking to the ears and necks of the other camels. The young males and other females move aside.

Tipu nudges the object of his desire and she shies away. He trots beside her as if he owns her. She breaks into a run, bleating insistently now, her eyes turning sideways, showing white. He lopes along next to her as she wades into a clump of yearlings. They scatter, and Tipu hooks his chin over her neck. They circle, the female bleating softly.

All pretense of protest gives way, and with a quick flick of her tail, she kneels down. He moves astride her back, his front legs over her shoulders. She nuzzles his neck, which arches over her head, and the foam from his mouth smears her ears, like soap when Dadi shaves.

I wonder if it's the same with humans. Do females want to be owned? I steal a look at Phulan and she knows what I'm thinking. She bursts out laughing.

"Don't worry, Shabanu!" she says, hugging me, and I hug her back, hard.

A deep bellow sounds from the far end of the *toba*. It is a huge young male Dadi plans to take to Sibi. Each herd has one dominant camel. Only he mates with the females. The others must suppress their ardor. If a young camel challenges the stud, they fight to the death.

Phulan and I hold our breath. If this young male, puffed up and full of himself, challenges Tipu, we will have to separate them or we could lose both of them.

Tipu responds with a roar. He leaves his lovemaking and stands, turning his head to look for his challenger.

Without a word, Phulan picks up the hem of her *chadr* and runs for Guluband to fetch Dadi, who is out gathering wood. I scramble to my feet and reach for the heavy stick I always carry.

Tipu, named after the great Indian warrior, has many battle scars from challenges like this. He spots the younger male, Kalu, which means "black." He is named for the great black camel Grandfather rode into battle for the Nawab of Bahawalpur. Kalu is larger than Tipu, and very strong, although he is only four years old.

Tipu roars again, lowers his head, and charges. Kalu is

ready with a deft feint. Tipu bumps him with his chest, but Kalu lowers his huge black head, ducks it under Tipu's chest, and clamps his powerful jaws around Tipu's foreleg.

I run at them, screaming at the top of my voice. But they don't even look up. I beat at their heads with my stick, hoping to distract them.

I am enormously relieved to hear Dadi shout to me to get away. He jumps off Guluband's back while the camel is still at a dead run. Phulan jumps down as soon as Guluband stops, and she and Dadi join me in trying to separate the fighting camels. Both camels are now thoroughly enraged and obsessed with the thought of killing.

Phulan and I beat our sticks against their sides with all our might. The sticks make solid thwacking sounds, but the camels seem not to notice, as we dance aside to keep away from their twisting necks and biting jaws. Both males' mouths are foaming pink with blood from cuts on their humps, necks, and legs. They whirl and heave, angling for advantage. They're so large that they seem to move with unnatural slowness, but Phulan and I have to run to keep up with them as they hurl each other about, the ground shaking under our feet, their roars reverberating in our chests.

The sweat runs down from under Dadi's turban, streaking his face. His mustache is coated with thick, pale dust. He tries to stay near the camels' heads, jabbing his stick into their faces as they thrash. There! He pushes the stick between Tipu's jaws.

"Get Kalu off!" he shouts, and Phulan and I slash at the young male's ribs with our sticks. Happy to have survived his unsuccessful challenge with dignity, Kalu lifts his head and trots away. Phulan and I turn our sticks to the big camel facing Dadi.

Diverted from the fight, Tipu seems to notice our blows for the first time and roars in protest, killing still the only thing on his mind. He shifts his fury to Dadi, whose stave is still jammed between Tipu's great jaws. The camel backs away and lowers his head, knocking the stick aside with a toss of his neck. His fierce eyes fix on Dadi's face. I run toward Tipu, screaming, my stick raised to strike at him, but he lowers his head again, preparing to lunge. My blow falls short by several feet, and I throw the stick at him with all my strength. He doesn't notice when it glances off his ribs.

Dadi locks his eyes steadily on the camel's, unwinding his turban as he backs slowly away. Tipu rubs a foot over the ground, swaying forward and back, building momentum for a charge. As he lunges, Dadi flings his turban into the camel's face and runs.

We're not far behind when Phulan's *chadr* twists about her legs. Tipu seizes the turban and shakes it furiously, his eyes wild with hatred. I turn back to Phulan and unwrap the black cloth, throwing it to the ground. She looks confused for a moment, but I grab her arm and run, and she stumbles to keep up with me.

I look back over my shoulder to see the camel toss back his brown domed head, shooting Dadi's turban into the air as if it had weight, then dashing it to the ground like a broken body. He falls on it with a roar so terrifying the female camels bolt, nudging their babies into the center of the gamboling herd.

Tipu pestles the turban to shreds in the sand with his knees and the pad on his mighty chest. We run like the hot summer wind over the hard-packed earth that surrounds the *toba,* our eyes blurred, the air whistling in our ears, feeling the shiny, cracked clay crunch under our feet.

Once we're beyond the *toba* bed, the shifting dunes suck at our feet as we scramble up the powdery sand, our progress dangerously slowed. Tipu is still venting his wrath on Dadi's turban, too absorbed to realize we've gotten away.

Phulan cries out and I turn in alarm, but it's Guluband trotting up behind us. Dadi twines his fingers into the camel's fur and swings up onto the long muscular neck. He pulls Phulan up behind him and reaches down for me.

"Mithoo!" I say, looking around for him.

"Don't be stupid," says Dadi. "Tipu isn't interested in him."

"I can't leave Mithoo alone," I protest. The females will shove him away. He'll be frightened.

Dadi reaches down and grabs my arm roughly, hauling me from my feet onto Guluband's back.

"No!" I scream, fighting to break his grip.

But Dadi clicks his tongue and commands *"Hunteray,"* and Guluband stretches into a long, loping gallop over the dunes, the sand glistening as it flies beneath us. I look behind and Tipu is smaller against the edge of the water, his head thrown back in a roar.

A hundred feet ahead I spot Mithoo, legs flailing as he runs, veering first to the left, then right, bleating like a little lamb, but headed in approximately the right direction. The brass bell on the red cord around his neck jangles wildly.

Dadi looks back at Tipu and orders Guluband to kneel. "Uuuussshh!" In three strides Dadi catches Mithoo, lifts him into his arms and carries him back. I throw my arms around Mithoo's neck and Dadi's, and we all come close to falling off as Guluband rises, back legs first, pitching us forward. Our heads bump, sending up clouds of dust. Phulan and I laugh with relief, but Dadi is silent.

Mama and Auntie run toward us, their long, bright skirts and *chadr*s flying out on the wind. Grandpa is far behind, hobbling on his stick. We meet them halfway to the settlement, and Guluband slows to a trot. Mama is gulping air as she reaches up and grasps Dadi's ankle before Guluband comes to a full halt. She lays her cheek against his foot.

"Thank God, thank God," she says over and over, tears running down her face. Mama seldom cries.

Guluband kneels and Dadi sets Mithoo down. He scampers away, and I am about to follow when Dadi turns and grabs me by the arms.

"Don't ever disobey me!" he says, shaking me so hard my head snaps back and forward, back and forward. His eyes are as furious as Tipu's, and I am speechless. He lets me go and walks away from us all without a word. For a moment we are frozen with shock and exhaustion. Then Mama breaks away and runs to catch up with Dadi's dust-streaked back.

That night as the air begins to cool and the desert colors fade after sunset, Mama, Auntie, Phulan, and I prepare dinner in the courtyard. My little cousins play hide-and-seek around the saddles, impatient to eat. Mama is silent as she stirs the spicy yellow lentils in our big copper pot, the firelight flickering on her face. I make the *chapatis*, and when Phulan and Auntie go outside she looks up at me.

"Shabanu, you are wild as the wind. You must learn to obey. Otherwise . . . I am afraid for you," she says, her face serious.

"But Mithoo . . ."

"In less than a year you'll be betrothed. You aren't a child anymore. You must learn to obey, even when you disagree." I am angry to think of Dadi or anyone else telling me what to do. I want to tell her I spend more time with the camels than Dadi, and sometimes when he asks me to do a thing, I know something else is better. But Mama's dark eyes hold my face so intently that I know she really is afraid for me, and I say nothing. She and Dadi are thinking of how I will behave when Murad and I marry.

Later the house is quiet. Mama is sewing by the last firelight, and Phulan is beside me under the quilt, sleeping. I lie still, thinking of Dadi's words.

Phulan is the one to be married. How can I forget, the way she arranges her *chadr* around her, languid and important with her new status?

Yesterday we bathed at the *toba*. I watched her secretly from behind the curtain of my own hair while Mama poured water over it. Phulan sat shamelessly naked to the waist, stroking her skin and running her long fingers through her wet hair. Her breasts have begun to poke out into tiny round swellings, each the size of a camel dropping. Her deep-set eyes looked far away.

I looked down at my own flat chest and my arms and legs, brown with the sun, short and rounded with muscle. My body is like Dadi's, as is my face—large black eyes, with a strong nose and a square chin.

Phulan looks like Mama, tall and slender, with golden eyes and fine features. Her face is open and alive when her fingers fly over the kneading bowl, as if she is trying to see into her new life at the edge of the desert. She smiles mysteriously through the dust clouds that rise from her broom of desert twigs, seeing the sons she'll bear Hamir.

I have no patience with housework. I rush through folding the quilts and sweeping, cross to be kept from my beloved camels. I mend harnesses and spin their hair into twine, watching the herd while the sun skids across the sky. I can't abide anything that keeps me from the animals, from running free and climbing thorn trees.

I have known Murad all my life. We've played together at our cousins' weddings. He is four years older than I am, and I always liked him for bothering to play with us.

Perhaps he did so because he could beat us at any game. The last time I saw him was in the fall at Adil's wedding. He's sixteen now, tall and serious, and still wants to win at games.

Dadi is a wise man, and I've never truly learned to obey him. How can I let a boy with a skinny neck and ears that stick out from under his turban tell me what to do?

The smell of smoldering embers is comforting. In the dying light the smoke climbs straight and narrow to the top of the thatch. I am about to fall asleep when I hear Dadi come in. There is rustling as Mama unrolls their quilt, and they undress.

"They're back at the *toba*," he says. "Everything seems quiet. Tipu is resting. The young male has gone away."

"You'll have to be careful," says Mama.

"I won't be able to turn my back on Tipu until I'm dead and buried," says Dadi, laughing.

"Can't you sell him before you leave?"

"Who'd buy him? He's thin as a stick from mating. I'll have to watch him every second until we get to Sibi. Such a shame. He won't fetch a good price, and yet he produces beautiful stock."

Shutr keena, "camel vengeance," is what it's called. One time a relative of Auntie's beat one of his camels. A year later the camel crushed the man's head in his jaws.

In the desert, men aren't so different from camels. They never leave an old argument unsettled. I soften some and begin to forgive Dadi's anger of this afternoon. In my heart I know he's trying to protect me.

Safari

We're ready to leave. My new dress makes me feel important. Guluband is handsome in his silver harness, polished to a glimmer. The other camels—fifteen in all—wear bright yellow, red, and green tassels, bells on leather harnesses around their necks, and bangles on their legs. They stamp their feet and groan, impatient for us to finish our farewells.

Dadi and Grandfather have clipped the fur on the

camels' flanks and sides into whorls and chevrons. Phulan and I have washed them in the *toba* and brushed them until they glisten. We have dyed the geometric designs black and made circles around their legs with henna.

There are seven males, including Tipu and the magnificent, malevolent Kalu. Once two males have fought, they never fight again. But we must not turn our backs on either one, for although the quarrel between them is settled, the grudge they bear against us is not.

The males are loaded with wooden saddles Grandfather has made for us to sell, gray camel-hair blankets trimmed with braided cord, quilts, a tent, cook pots, water, lentils, and wheat flour. Two young males carry new babies in panniers on their backs, and the mothers stand beside their flanks, their noses just touching the little ones. We've tied the udders of two milking females with goat-hair mesh bags.

I have kissed Mama and Auntie good-bye and instructed Phulan to find Mithoo a mother to nurse him. As I hug his neck, he nuzzles me, greedy to find the lump of brown sugar I've hidden from morning tea. Grandfather stands like a shadow in the half-light, his hands raised in wordless farewell. There seems nothing left to say. Dadi wants to be off well before sunup, for even in mid-February the noonday sun bakes you until you are consumed with desire for water.

Auntie disappears into her hut and returns with a cloth

folded in her hands. Solemnly she shakes it out and drapes it around my head and shoulders.

"A young lady shouldn't go with her head uncovered. You're too old to act like a boy," says Auntie. I yank it away and she presses her lips together into a thin line. Mama lays a hand on Auntie's arm.

"Shabanu, it matches your new dress," says Mama, pleading with her eyes. "It'll keep the sun off your head." She picks up the *chadr* and lays it again over my hair and shoulders. She takes my face in her hands and kisses it, and looks straight into my eyes. I look up at Dadi, already on Guluband's back, reins in his hands. He looks straight ahead.

"Thank you, Auntie," I say, wanting to curse her. Auntie repeats a message for her husband, whom Dadi will see in Rahimyar Khan, that he should send new brass water pots.

Dadi reaches down and hauls me up behind him, and Guluband lurches to his feet without waiting for a command. The dark blue cloth slips to my shoulders. I push back my clean and newly plaited hair and make no effort to adjust the *chadr*.

"*Hunteray,*" says Dadi. Guluband shakes his great shaggy head and steps out, and our little caravan is under way.

For the first half hour Dadi and I talk little. We see a herd of black buck, their horns spiraling skyward like smoke. Dadi stands in front of Guluband's hump to watch them, and I stand behind, holding onto his shoulders. They sail over a dry *toba*, delicate legs tucked up under them, their horns perpendicular to the earth in the magical, opalescent moment before sunrise.

Dadi jumps down to walk and check the camels behind. Guluband senses I am alone on his back and turns his ears. Softly, so Dadi can't hear, I sing a few lines.

> *Friday market, what's for sale?*
> *Melons, onions, and fat oxtail.*
> *Sell me your camel strong and brave?*
> *Not for a million rupees, knave!*

Guluband picks up his legs, his bracelets keeping beat with my voice, *kachinnik, kachinnik, kachinnik.* Dadi joins our song, making up a question in his clear, rich voice for me to answer and Guluband to dance to across the desert.

> *Won't you sell me a baby lamb?*
> *On the hoof or in the pan?*
> *Buy my motorcycle, sir?*
> *Better sell me a coat of fur!*

Waves of heat shimmer upward, and mirage lakes glisten among the dunes ahead. We slow our pace, and Guluband's rocking gait lulls me. Dadi and I take turns walking, making sure the younger camels keep up. The air is hot, but a steady breeze cools our skin. And Mama is right—the *chadr* keeps the sun from my head.

We pass Maujgarh Fort, destroyed by time and the feet of thousands of goats, sheep, cows, and children. Nearly half of the dome high above the fort's walls has fallen since we passed this way last year. Piles of rubble have accumulated at the base of the walls, and inside the half dome, beams stick out in silhouette at odd angles, like broken limbs. A few blue tiles still cling to the pinkish brick hemisphere.

Night falls and we press on to Derawar Fort, where Grandfather fought for the Nawab of Bahawalpur as a young man. Dadi keeps the guiding star on his shoulder. The camels always know where they are. We never worry about being lost.

Dadi leaves me near the south wall to set up camp while he makes his *salaam*s to the villagers and the Desert Rangers.

A half-moon and the stars light my way to search the heavy brush for wild sage to feed the camels and tumbling clumps of *pogh* for a fire to make *chapati*s and tea.

The camels are hobbled and lie contentedly, their noses over their dinners. I am kneading dough in a wooden bowl when Dadi returns. He looks happy as he squats to feed the fire.

After we have eaten, we sit quietly, discussing how we should redistribute our load in the morning. The fire flickers golden on his face, with its strong, square chin and mustache that turns up at the ends, and I think he is more handsome than any soldier in the world.

The camels grunt, and we hear footfalls outside the circle of our firelight. Three Ranger officers in gray baggy trousers and starched tunics with red shoulder boards step into the glow. Their eyes are hard with the difficulties of life in the desert. Yet, like us, they wouldn't live anywhere else.

They are desert men trained by the Pakistan Army to patrol the Indian border. When one of our people is sick, the Rangers' doctor comes from Yazman, an hour away by jeep track. The Rangers also help find our animals when they stray across the border.

"Asalaam-o-Aleikum," says the oldest of the three, touching his fingertips to his forehead and heart in a formal Cholistan greeting. Their shirts are loose; without their black berets and belts with silver ornaments and buckles, they must be relaxing, just passing time after supper.

"Are you headed for Sibi?" asks the leader. He is tall and very strong looking, but his eyes are gentle.

I whisk milk and sugar into tea over the fire for our guests as Dadi tells them the route we'll take to Sibi: We will spend tomorrow in the desert. Around nightfall we will reach the Khanpur irrigation canal, and our third night we will spend near Rahimyar Khan. Next day we'll cross the Indus River back into the desert and the tribal area of Baluchistan. We will wait there to join other nomads, for the tribal territory can be dangerous, and crossing in numbers is safest.

"We hope to reach Sibi in ten days, God willing," Dadi tells the Rangers.

Two of the Rangers inspect the camels by flashlight.

They return to the fire and motion to their leader. I look at Dadi, hoping they aren't going to tell us we can't pass through the area, but he sits calmly, watching the fire and sipping his tea.

They talk softly as they shine their light from one animal to the next. We keep our camels clean and well fed. None of them has a trace of mange. Everyone admires them.

"My men say your camels are extremely fine," says the leader. They stand beside Guluband, whose proud head towers over the others.

"I'll give you eight thousand rupees for this one," the leader says.

Dadi, who has been deferential and extremely polite with the Rangers, throws back his head and laughs loudly.

"The Afghan *mujahideen* will give me twelve in a minute," he says.

My heart thunders in my chest. Surely Dadi won't sell Guluband! Our finest camel, who dances for me and waits patiently in the hot sun and stays near when I may need him! We've had him ever since I can remember.

The men return to the fire. Dadi eyes me, and I pour more tea into their cups.

"You don't want to sell such a fine beast to the *mujahideen*," says the officer.

"They offer the best price," says Dadi, shrugging his shoulders. My hands tremble and I stare at Dadi, willing him to see into my heart and know I will die if he sells Guluband.

"But you know what they do to them?" asks the officer. "They load them with guns and take them across the border. They beat them and don't feed them. They haven't any idea how to treat animals. And the Russians fly over in helicopters, shooting every pack animal. A camel like that might last one or two trips. It would be a waste," he says, shaking his head.

I can't bear it. I manage to stand quietly and back away from the fire. Dadi doesn't look up, but I can tell he is watching through the edge of his vision. I turn and run blindly. Thorns grab at my skirt and sink into my bare feet. I run until I reach the wall of the fort, and lay my face and hands against its bricks, still warm from the afternoon sun.

My eyes adjust slowly to the desert starlight. There are no shadows, and the stars illuminate everything to an equal intensity. Nothing has color, only infinite shades of brightest light and blackest dark, but even insects are visible in the sand.

I walk, making a circle around the huge fort, leaving our camp and the sleeping village behind. Back beyond the ancient mosque is a garden, where it is said the Abassi prince kept seventy wives in richly decorated underground cells. Standing outside the sagging wooden gate, I look into the now overgrown garden and imagine dozens of jeweled consorts laughing and singing under the trees, pulling silken veils over mysterious smiles. Prisoners, willingly or unwillingly they lived their lives according to the wishes of their fathers and their prince.

Dadi is snoring in his bedroll when I return. The fire barely flickers as I check the animals. Guluband nuzzles me gently, looking for a piece of sugar.

I take an onion from our bag of provisions. I peel away several strips of skin, tying a piece inside my hem and putting the others at the corners of Dadi's bedroll to keep the scorpions away. I spread my own quilt on the ground and immediately fall into a deep sleep. Several times in the night Tipu roars in protest at being tethered.

In the morning we go to the beautiful old mosque built by the Nawab behind the fort. The latticed marble balustrades and intricate tiled floor already are warm in the pink and golden predawn light. I know I mustn't pray to Allah for Guluband, but I keep him in my heart as I whisper along with Dadi when he recites from the Koran.

During the next days my mind is blank as the sky. The scrub and dunes give way to the dank, green irrigated area. Dadi and I talk only when it concerns the track or the animals. We pass along a road crowded with camels carrying mountains of sugarcane and bullock carts that clatter and jingle. In the fields women harvest winter wheat, their heads covered with colored shawls bobbing like bright flowers in the wind. Bedford trucks and buses painted like large luminescent beetles part the mist with a roar.

Dadi has not said we will sell Guluband, but I dare not ask. I know he's our best camel and we need the money for the wedding.

We spend one night near a village. Dadi is gone when I awake. It's after sunup when he returns. Mist rises from the canal, and the acrid smoke of cow dung fires from the nearby village burns my eyes and throat. He hands me a long, round paper bundle and lifts his chin, signaling me to open it. I tear away the thin brown paper and hear tinkling inside a second layer of newspaper wrapping.

Glass bangles! Blue to match my dress, red to match the flowers on it, green for the ribbon on my hem.

"They're beautiful—all the right colors!" He smiles happily as I slip them over my wrist. They make glistening bands of color halfway to my elbow, and I shake them gently to hear them clink.

The Bugtis

My chest tightens as we near the Gudu Barrage, an irrigation dam upon which we cross the mighty Indus River. The road is choked with speeding buses, trucks, and cars, horns blasting as if the Indus hasn't blocked men's paths for thousands of years. The camels are nervous, turning their heads from side to side to watch the vehicles hurtle past. Grunts and roars sound through the caravan as we walk carefully, the camels swaying along the edge of the seething road.

Under us, the river is brown and muddy. It looks lazy and slow-moving, but the powerful current sucks at the pediments of the dam and swirls before breaking around barriers that force the water into separate channels.

Later we meet another caravan that has stopped beneath a stand of thorn trees. They also are Cholistani nomads, three men dressed in white *lungi*s and tunics and plaid turbans. Dadi embraces them, and we sit under a tree where the oldest, a crooked, sinewy man, lights an old brass filigree *hookah* pipe filled with tobacco and brown sugar. They offer the snakelike mouthpiece to Dadi first. He pulls the smoke, bubbling softly through water in the *hookah* base, into his lungs.

The men agree to travel together. The Baluch are unpredictable people. In Grandfather's time the Bugtis and Marris and other tribes of Baluchistan lived in the barren hills and earned their living by plundering in the fertile Punjabi plains. Now their lives are very much like ours— they herd goats, sheep, and camels. Mostly they know we are poorer than they are. Sometimes they are hospitable, otherwise they just leave us alone.

But in times of unrest no outsider is welcome in the tribal lands, where the only law is God's.

We are on our way again. Dadi is pleased to have the company of other men, and I ride quietly, listening to them gossip.

The sun is fierce, heating the rocks that loom over the track like a bread oven. By midafternoon I am possessed by the thought of water. Guluband sweats, and my nostrils are filled with the strong smell of the urine of thirsty camels. After today, they will have no water for the three remaining days to Sibi.

I doze, lulled by the graceful forward and back motion of Guluband's gait. The caravan stops, jolting me awake. On the ridge beside the trail at eye level stands a band of Bugtis, a breeze filling their voluminous trousers and shirtsleeves. My heart leaps into my mouth. Their chests are crossed with bandoliers. Their eyes are fierce between long beards and intricately wound turbans. Several of them lean on long, brass-studded rifles.

Dadi and one of our new companions climb slowly up the rocks, their hands open, palms up in humble greeting. The Bugtis don't return the salute.

"*Asalaam-o-Aleikum*," says Dadi in his fine, clear voice. "We are nomads from Cholistan, taking our camels, God willing, to the great Sibi Fair. We beg your permission to pass this place in peace."

I am dizzy with holding my breath. How does Dadi know one of them won't shoot him?

An old man with skin sun-stained the color of rosewood steps forward. His beard is white, the end dyed bright red with henna.

"I am Sardar Nothani Bugti," he says in a deep voice younger than his years. "We are looking for my brother's

43

daughter. She has eloped with a Marri tribesman. If you are not protecting her, then you can go in peace, and God go with you."

"My daughter is the only female with us, and she is just a child," says Dadi, his voice calm.

For the first time in my life, I pull the *chadr* over my face and lower my head beneath the gaze of these men.

When we are under way again, Dadi comes back and walks by Guluband's side, his hand resting on my foot.

"You know, little one," he says, "these men will kill the woman when they find her."

I don't answer. He is reminding me that I must abide by the rules.

Two or three other caravans are already camped at the foot of the Bugti hills. I take Guluband and the other camels to a small stream and let the cool water run over my feet.

After a dinner of tea and *chapati*s, plus a bit of dried meat, Dadi joins the men around the fire, sucking at *hookah*s, comparing what they've heard about Sibi this year. The prices are good, they say.

"The Afghan *mujahideen* are paying twelve thousand rupees for the really good camels," says the old man whose caravan we joined earlier in the day.

"Oh, the Afghans pay nothing compared to the Iranians," says an old Baluch herdsman whose village is nearby. The other men turn to him, and for a second the *hookah*s are silent.

"The government fixed a priced of fifteen hundred dollars on breeding stock a few years ago," he says, leaning forward.

"But that was only for dancing and fighting camels going to Saudi Arabia for breeding," says Dadi. "You need papers, and they're hard to come by."

"You must pay off officials to get such papers," says a young Cholistani. "If I sold my whole herd, maybe I could come up with the payoff." The others laugh.

"Nay, nay," says the Baluch, persistent. "The Iranians and many Arabs prefer to sacrifice camels for the feast of *Eid*. They like camel meat better than anything. And they have heard we export camels for fifteen hundred dollars—not rupees."

The men are silent, and the dinner I've eaten rises in a lump to the top of my stomach. We slaughter goats for *Eid*, the Muslim feast that follows the holy fasting month of Ramadan. The thought of cutting the throat of one of our magnificent camels and watching its blood disappear without a trace into the sand, the animal thrashing until its heart is dry, is unbearable. I hold my breath, unable to move as the talk goes on.

"We may be poor, but we love our animals," says Dadi. "Why else would we live in the desert?" My heart lifts with hope that he won't sell our camels to Arabs for meat.

The men around the fire are too polite to express disbelief, but they sit quietly, sucking at the *hookah*s.

"You'll see I'm right," says the Baluch.

I am numb. Last year at Sibi Dadi refused all offers for

Guluband. He danced, showing off at the gentlest urging. He stood a head taller than the thousands of other camels at the fair. Everyone had agreed he was the finest camel at Sibi. Dadi had turned down an offer of fifteen thousand rupees for him. I must believe this year will be the same.

Sibi Fair

My heart is lighter when we reach the railway track, and I dream of where it comes from and where it goes, to Quetta at the edge of the Sulaiman Range, which rises north to the Hindu Kush Mountains of Afghanistan, and south to Karachi, the big city on the Arabian Sea. Such places it passes through! We follow the glistening ribbons for several hours.

My heart quickens as we turn off the main road, and

ahead the fairground is engulfed in a swirl of dust. I sit up high on Guluband's hump to watch people of all kinds: tribesmen wearing the striped turbans of the Marris, the Bugtis in billowy trousers and embroidered vests, mountain men carrying guns of every size and description. Elaborately decorated animals crowd together as far as I can see: bullocks with humps dyed shocking pink, their horns garlanded with yellow tassels, black horses covered by red blankets stitched with cotton puffs and mirrors, and camels so numerous their humps look like part of the hills that stretch into Afghanistan.

A small boy in bare feet runs along beside us, leading us to the place where we will camp and buyers will inspect our animals and haggle over prices.

Here and there men with rough wooden scales surrounded by mounds of green weigh fodder for sale. Men stand under fringed umbrellas selling cold drinks that sparkle red and yellow in the sun. Other men turn huge red wheels, crushing sugarcane, the juice oozing out into large, dirty glasses. There are no women, only a few girls of my age and younger.

The tangy smell of fresh animal excrement and the sweet smell of the freshly cut fodder are familiar and exciting. My mouth waters with the thought of the sugarcane. Guluband is excited too, shaking his big head, growling like a camel in rut.

I can't wait to get to the carnival, but I must first tether and unpack the camels and brush the dust and mud from their fur and clean their feet. I must make our camp, build a fire, and fix something to eat. It will be hours before I can slip away to the carnival. Dadi helps me with the heavy loads, whistling through his teeth and talking to the animals.

"Dadi," I ask, "were you frightened by the Bugtis?"

He turns, a sack of wheat flour on his shoulder.

"Perhaps at the time, but I felt Allah willed we would be safe."

"Do you think if you believe something hard enough, it will happen?" Or not happen, is what I really want to ask.

He laughs and plops the sack down into the circle of our belongings that defines our camp. I have already spread the reed mats on the ground, leaving a large open space in the center for a fire.

"I just know that whatever Allah wills, it will be so. And there's no reason to be afraid, because what Allah wills cannot be changed."

He holds my face in his hands and looks into my eyes.

"So. After the sun goes down I'll take you to the carnival. God will take care of everything." I hug him until he laughs and pries me loose.

He opens my hand and piles five one-rupee notes and a small mound of change on my palm. I've never had so much to spend! I jump up and down, and it scatters in the dust at my feet.

"Shabanu," says Dadi, a warning in his voice.

But he shakes his head and smiles again and helps me gather up my booty. I tie it into one corner of my *chadr* and wrap it close to my body, the bundle clutched in my hand. He hands me a hundred-rupee note, and Guluband and I go off to buy fodder for the animals.

I ride Guluband down the main avenue of the fairground, past rows and rows of animals and men sitting on empty oxcarts talking prices. They all look up to see such a fine animal, and I lift my chin and look straight ahead. I think this, even more than the carnival, is what I look forward to from year to year. How I'll miss it next year. I try to imagine myself a veiled woman with a family of my own. A shiver steals across my shoulders.

After Guluband and I return with the fodder, I feed the animals, all the while running back to be sure that the tea kettle is full and that the prospective buyers have tea. It seems forever until Dadi asks our traveling companion, who is camped next to us, to watch the animals so we can go to the carnival. I'm grateful—it's late and Dadi hasn't even eaten.

He lifts me to his shoulders so I can see everything, and we walk through the fairground. At the main gate we turn right, and a large wooden arch covered with pinwheels of colored lights blinks a welcome to the carnival.

Inside the air is choked with dust. Music blends with laughter, shouting, and the roar of motorcycles from the daredevil pit. Ahead is a platform around which painted wooden horses with tinsel manes and tails move up and down on poles as the platform spins to the music of a pipe organ and drum. Dadi sets me down and I pay several annas for a ride.

I grasp the pole, and the ponies whirl and whirl, and buck up and down like a new horse being broken. My heart hammers. When the platform slows I'm more excited and pleased than relieved. I want another ride.

"We'll come back," says Dadi, his eyes flashing as he takes my hand. "I'll show you something better: the big wheel!"

We push through the crowd, men jammed so tight their shoulders touch. On Dadi's shoulders again, I see it—the big wheel looming beyond a sea of turbans, buckets dangling from its edge as it spins in a blur, the mirrored scarves of young girls flying like flags.

A man climbs the scaffolding to the hub of the wheel six times his height from the ground. At the top he lunges into the air and grabs a bar sticking out from the side of the wheel, and the force of his weight spins it around. As he nears the bottom of the arc he jumps to the ground and scrambles up the scaffolding again. The wheel spins faster and faster, until the man tires, and the wheel stops to let off breathless passengers and take on another group of people who have been waiting their turn.

Our mouths are dry as we sit in a vacant bucket and the man snaps a bar in place over our legs. He perspires heavily in the cool evening air. He climbs the scaffolding and grabs the bar and we fly into the air, our stomachs at the backs of our throats, then plummet down again at a speed that seems certain to dash us to the ground. I am dizzy, and my stomach feels out of place when the ride is over.

"You need a *paan* to settle your stomach," says Dadi. I've never had one—usually only grownups eat betel, and I'm pleased Dadi has offered it. I climb back onto his shoulders, and we head into the crowd again.

We stop beside a large red wagon painted with flowers and animals—tigers and elephants and giant birds. In the center of the wagon bed sits a woman in a seductive pose, swaying her shoulders and dipping her head. I am shocked, though her scarf is draped demurely over her face. She watches me with one smiling eye as she reaches into a plate of water and retrieves a fresh betel leaf.

"You like it sweet?" she asks in a voice that is both surprisingly deep and as syrupy as the thick sugar water with rose petals in it that she spreads over the leaf. She winks her painted eye and lays a thin sheet of silver on top of the rose water.

Next she sprinkles white powder and crushed flower petals and some colored crystals and mysterious-looking withered shreds over the leaf. With deft fingers she wraps the whole thing into a neat triangle, tucks in the edges, and leans over to hand it to me.

Her scarf slips to reveal breasts that look hard and pointed under her dress. She jangles her silver bracelets and flutters her fingers. I peer more closely into her face. A tiny stubble of beard peeps through the white powder on her chin.

I gasp and step back. With a gravelly giggle, she re-wraps her scarf and holds out a long, slender hand with black hairs on the knuckles for a rupee.

I marvel at the wickedness of this man-woman. The *paan* is delicious, and I feel very grown up.

We get stuck in a crowd standing outside a tent, the men's eyes on a deformed midget dancing, his hips and shoulders undulating to a rhythm played by two musicians pumping at tuneless instruments. A man in a filthy tunic promises through a microphone that the dancing inside is performed by beautiful women who do forbidden things. Dadi pushes through the immobile crowd, pulling me away.

Half the money Dadi has given me is gone, and the evening breeze sways the colored lights strung overhead. It's past the time we should get back. Unwillingly I let Dadi pull me by the hand toward the pinwheel gate. I ask if I can come back tomorrow to watch the man in tights lift the five-hundred-pound barbells, and the daredevil cyclists ride circles upside down through a flaming cylinder, and the wrestlers.

When we return to our camp, four strangers with guns are waiting. Their leader is a one-eyed Pathan whom Dadi greets, calling him Wardak. One of the others has only one arm. I have never seen such wild-looking men.

Dadi gestures me away, so I go to search for the bowl and pan to make *chapatis*. I start the fire, make tea with lots of sugar and milk, and leave it resting on a stone at the edge of the fire. But Dadi doesn't offer them tea.

I keep my eyes on the men as I feed the animals and knead dough. They all wear huge gray turbans, wound in a way I've never seen before. Their shoes are dirty and worn. They look very sinister. Wardak gestures angrily. He turns his back on Dadi as if to walk away. Dadi stands still and silent. I wish I can hear what they're saying!

Wardak turns back again toward Dadi, and Dadi shakes his head. After a while they leave, and Dadi watches their backs for a moment before coming to the fire. It's way past time for us to be in bed, and the *chapati*s are cold.

"What do they want?" I ask, my voice little more than a whisper. "They're Afghans, aren't they?"

Dadi nods. He is drawing figures in the dirt by the fire with a stick. Mama has taught me the little reading she knows, but I can't make out what he's writing.

"Dadi, tell me, please," I say.

"Shabanu, we could be very rich in another week. You and Phulan would have fine weddings and dowries that would stand you well for the rest of your lives." He smiles, but his eyes are sad, and I have an empty feeling in my stomach that presses outward as if I'll burst.

"Please don't sell Guluband," I whisper, looking down at the fire. "Please, please, please."

"I won't if I can help it," he says.

"But the others," I say. "What you told the Baluch, that you'd rather sell them for meat than have them abused and shot down by soldiers!"

"I know," he says. "Others are interested in the whole herd, too. I've asked the Afghans to pay twice what they're willing to pay. Don't worry, little one."

That night, as I clean the pans and put them away, other men come to the fire to talk to Dadi. Just as last year, they are most interested in Guluband. Dadi tells them he isn't for sale.

Dadi keeps the fire going far into the night. I am comforted that he'd told so many he won't sell Guluband for any price, and I sleep soundly. I wake occasionally to Tipu's lovesick roars, and when buyers come to try to persuade Dadi with offers that grow higher and higher, he refuses, and happily I fall back to sleep.

Next morning Guluband and I go to buy fodder. We return to find Dadi talking to Wardak and the one-armed man. Dadi listens, his back toward me. When Wardak finishes speaking, there is a long silence until Dadi speaks.

"Twenty-eight thousand for the big one, twenty-two for the other males, fifteen for each female, twenty for the pregnant ones, and eight apiece for the small ones. That's two hundred seventy-six thousand, and not a paisa less."

Wardak spits in the dust and walks away. I drop the twenty kilos of fodder Guluband and I have carried from the vendor and jump to the ground.

"You said you wouldn't" I shout, sobs tearing through my voice.

Dadi grabs me by the arms and shakes me hard until I'm quiet.

"Hush! He'll never pay that much. And if he does, I don't want a word out of you."

I cry out and yank my arms away from him. He lets me go and I run blindly, my *chadr* flying out behind me, all the way to the canal that borders the fairground. I can't stay long. I know Dadi can't leave the animals alone with that man wanting Guluband so much. I sit hugging me knees, staring into the gray water, searching for an answer.

I think of taking Guluband myself, but there is nowhere a girl can go safely alone. I think of the Bugti girl who loved the Marri boy, and of her father looking for them to kill her. I have no money, I know nobody outside my family. I have no choice but to obey Dadi and hope the Afghan won't pay that price for the whole herd.

When I get back to the camp, Dadi is showing the pregnant females to another buyer, a man in a huge white turban, with a big belly, enormous hands, and kind eyes. I ask if they want tea. Dadi looks at me and there is compassion in his eyes. I know I must remain in Dadi's good graces—it's my only hope.

The man comes into the camp and I hand them each a cup. The man thanks me and sits, sipping the tea noisily. He too is a Pathan, a herder from Zhob in north Baluchistan near the Afghanistan border. He tells Dadi half his herd was wiped out last year by disease. He needs good, strong females.

"The pregnant ones are each seven thousand," says Dadi. "I'll take six for each of the other females. Two have calves, and they must stay together. The calves are two thousand each."

My breath rushes in sharply. That's less than half the price Dadi has offered Wardak. Still the prices are high, and no doubt this man will bargain him down. Perhaps Dadi is right: Wardak will never pay that much!

The Bargain

The next morning the man from Zhob comes for breakfast. We sit around the warmth of the fire, eating in companionable silence as the sun comes up, spreading its watery light over the fairground.

When we have finished, the man sucks his teeth and stands.

"I've raised all I can. Thirty thousand."

"That will cover all but the milking female and one

other," says Dadi, standing so his eyes are level with the other man's.

"Your prices are the highest at Sibi," says the other.

"My camels are the best," Dadi replies. "Otherwise you'd put your thirty thousand on ten scrawny females from Sind."

The other man nods slowly.

"Let me give you twenty-four and leave out a pregnant female. They're always a risk."

Dadi chews on a piece of straw for a moment and tosses it into the fire.

"The two pregnant ones are the best females. You'll have no trouble. Both are a month from delivery. You're talking of false economy."

"But I need more . . ."

"One of the females hasn't dropped a calf in three years," says Dadi. "I want you to have my camels. You'll look after them well, and they'll produce fine calves and plenty of milk. If you have a good stud, the younger ones will give you a calf a year over the next seven years. Leave me the old dry one, and for your thirty thousand I'll sell you the other females and calves."

The man's face brightens. He has a good bargain. He lifts his tunic to pull several handfuls of crumpled notes from a canvas money belt. He sticks a huge forefinger inside to make sure no bills are left hiding.

He and Dadi shake hands and the deal is done. There is tea, a little gossip about other camel sellers, and more sucking of teeth before the man leads away all but one of the females.

Dadi smiles broadly as he turns back to the fire.

"This is a good beginning," he says, tugging my hair. I pour us each another cup of tea.

Later in the morning the dust rises, and Dadi is busy with a man who wants to buy Tipu. I sell two of Grandfather's saddles for three hundred rupees apiece. Dadi is so pleased he sends me out to buy two chickens for dinner and invites our caravan companions for a meal tonight.

When I return, he has sold Tipu for eighteen thousand! He is singing and laughing to himself when I come back with sacks of vegetables and the chickens.

"I'll go back and get two more chickens!" says Dadi, his turban pushed back on his head. "What luck! Eight camels!" It costs twenty rupees a day apiece just to feed them. And I don't think even Dadi expected to get such good prices.

I spend the rest of the day peeling onions and making curry and *chapati*s, fetching water from the canal and keeping the tea boiling for a stream of prospective buyers. Dadi and I begin to sing again, and he promises to take me tomorrow to see the daredevil and for another *paan*.

Late in the afternoon the wind comes up. A dust storm is building, and I scurry to put out the fire and find lids for the pots to keep the sand out, and a cloth to tie up the *chapati*s.

The wind whips my skirt and hair. The *chadr* and shawl together don't keep the sand from biting my skin. My teeth are gritty, and I open my eyes just wide enough to keep from tripping as I struggle to secure the tarpaulin to protect us and our belongings.

The camels shift positions to face into the wind. Their ears swivel back and their nostrils pinch down. They continue to ruminate with their eyes shut, content as old women in front of a fire.

I have secured three corners of the tarpaulin, and the last corner whips me about like a tassel on the end of a string. Dadi returns to help, and we drag sacks of flour, rice, and lentils under the tarpaulin. When we finally get underneath ourselves, every inch of my skin feels rubbed raw from the blowing sand. I fall asleep with the wind howling.

I am awakened by someone shouting "Abassi! Abassi!"

Dadi rises and goes outside. I lift a corner of the tarpaulin. Standing square into the wind is Wardak, looking like a wild man, with fire shooting out of his one good eye. He is alone. Dadi reties his turban tightly to secure it against the wind as he approaches Wardak.

The Afghan gestures furiously, and Dadi stands as he stood before, watching quietly. I sense Wardak is no stranger to killing. Dadi makes no move to invite him inside. The wind tears at them, plastering Dadi's shirt against his broad back and his *lungi* against his muscular legs.

Rain begins to fall in dense plops on the tarpaulin and

ground, sending up little splashes of mud. Still they stand outside, shouting above the storm.

The wind is frigid, and the rain beats in against my hands and face. My eyes are riveted on Wardak, who lifts his tunic and reaches into a canvas pouch hanging at his waist. He pulls out three bundles of stiff, blue five-hundred-rupee notes, still stapled together at one end. One hundred and fifty thousand rupees. Dadi's shoulder dips as he reaches for the notes. I can't see his hands or face.

I lift the flap higher and squeeze over a sack of rice. Wardak is halfway to where the camels are tethered when finally I can get a sound out of my paralyzed throat.

"No-o-o-o-o-o!" I scream, running at Wardak through the rain.

Dadi catches me halfway between the tent and Guluband, and he scoops me up in one arm. I kick at him and beat at the air.

"You promised!" I shriek. "Liar. You lied!"

Wardak has untethered the male camels, and Guluband is just getting to his feet.

"No-o-o-o!" I wail.

Dadi sets me down, and I try to break away from him. He holds me firmly by the arm. I bite at him like a wild animal. With his free hand he slaps my face, sending me to my knees. He still holds my arm.

Dadi's eyes are on Wardak as he leads the animals away.

"Guluband!" I shout. My voice is like glass shattering and falling to the ground in splinters.

Guluband turns his great shaggy head and fixes me for

a second with one clear brown eye. With a roar he turns, following Wardak obediently.

As I watch them disappear into the dim light, I know without a doubt that my heart is crumbling up inside me like a burning piece of paper. I sag against Dadi. He holds me against him for a moment, then lifts me in his arms and carries me into the tent.

Both of us are soaked and shivering. Dadi hands me a towel and tells me to take off my wet clothes. I obey, and he wraps me in a quilt, then goes out.

The wind dies, and the rain is now a gentle patter on the tarpaulin. I am numb and mute. Everything registers, but I cannot move. Dadi returns, folds back one edge of the tarpaulin, and builds a fire. I follow him with my eyes as he moves about the tent, arranging our clothes around the fire to dry and putting a kettle of tea on to boil.

He brings me a cup, but the salty-sweet tea turns bitter in my mouth and I choke. He takes back the cup. My teeth begin to chatter, and Dadi carries me to the fire. In its light, he inspects my face, looking at where he slapped me. I stare into his eyes, and for the first time he meets my look. He brushes his fingers over my tangled hair and folds me into his arms, where he holds me until I stop shivering.

When the rain stops and our clothes are dry, Dadi removes the stiff tarpaulin and folds it away. People begin to move around outside. I can hear the mud sucking at their feet. Dadi pushes the sacks of grains and pulses back into a big circle and covers the ground again with the reed mats.

He gets out the pots of curried chicken and lentils and rice and vegetables, and arranges them around the fire.

"Shabanu?" he says. I nod and take over the rest of the cooking while he goes out to find plates and cups to feed the men he has invited to celebrate the sale of our camels.

I feel strangely normal. I am not angry. I see everything clearly, as if I am awake for the first time in a long while. We are richer than we ever have been. From the sale of fourteen camels, Dadi has made enough for Phulan's wedding and dowry and for mine next year. He and Mama will have an easier life. They still have a fine herd of camels at home.

But at the center of my self is an aching hole. With Guluband, my joy, my freedom, all of who I am has gone. I wonder if I will ever take pleasure in anything again.

Dadi returns with a sackful of red clay cups and plates. With him are two men, one with a drum, the other with a tattered old bagpipe. They kick off their muddy sandals and line them up outside the circle of our camp.

The sky clears just as the sun sets. Dadi heaps wood on the fire in a pit surrounded by the dry, clean mats, and orange glints curve around the edges of the pots and the folds of the men's turbans.

The man with the bagpipe is the old man who shared his *hookah* with Dadi. He fills his frail frame with air and pumps up the bag. The sound begins as a low moan and rises as the pipes fill in an ancient tribal wail, the skin drum beating its rhythm underneath. Another man comes with a bamboo flute, and another with a roast leg of mutton.

Word spreads among the people of our caravan of Dadi's great sales, and each comes, bringing what he can to help celebrate, and also in the hope that our good fortune portends his own.

Shatoosh

My heart stands still for a moment when Wardak appears. I want to tear out his one eye and spit in its bloody socket. But the dull ache around the hole where my heart used to be leaves me drained of all energy. Wardak has brought a roasted lamb. Our companions greet him warmly. They respect his wealth.

The men deposit their tributes around the fire and squat in a circle to gossip about the camel selling. The buyers curse the Afghans for driving prices up. The sellers mention the possibility of driving their camels through the Makran Range into the hands of the camel-eating Iranians and Arabs. The music pulses and everyone waits to eat.

Dadi passes out the clay plates. There aren't enough. More appear. Trays heaped with meat, lentils, *chapatis*, vegetables, and rice are passed. I refill the teakettle again and again, moving about as if in a dream. Wardak never once looks in my direction.

After the men have eaten, the drummer quickens the rhythm of the music. Several men form a circle around the fire, smiling and swaying at first, then dipping and turning to clap their hands overhead, their steps a halting beat behind the drum in a traditional desert dance.

A young man who traveled with us through the Bugti tribal land tosses off his shawl and puts a reed between his lips. He lifts his arms gracefully and strikes at the air with his hands to staccato whistles through the reed, swaying like a mesmerized cobra. His feet lift forward quickly and smoothly, in time with the music and the reed. The others stand back, the fire flickering on their white tunics and turbans as they clap and whoop. A small boy joins in the snake dance, and the watching men twirl rupees over the dancers' turbans to ward off the evil eye.

Four men drag Dadi to the fire. Their hero for today must dance, but he must appear to be unwilling. Wardak tosses Dadi a sword. He catches it by the handle and hes-

itates for a moment. With a shout, another of our caravan mates leaps into the circle of the fire, his sword raised
over his head. The circle moves back farther, and the
drummer beats the tempo still faster. Dadi and the other
man whirl, duck, and leap in an intricate rhythm of hollow rings as their deadly swords flash in time to the tribal
drum. When it's over the two men sag exhausted against
each other, swords upraised, and the crowd cheers.

Outside the circle, the night is cold. The storm has
cleared the air, and the fairground is washed white with
moonlight. I can barely hear the mechanical noise of the
carnival above the music and voices. Half the fairground
seems to have gathered around our camp.

When the men have drifted away, I gather up the clay
dishes and cups, most of which lie broken around the edge
of the mats. We pack up some of what's left of the food
and distribute the rest among the people camped about
us.

Dadi looks tired, and his clothes are wrinkled and
sweaty.

I'm glad to be occupied with practical things as I mea-
sure out wheat and lentils for the trip home. The rest we'll
sell in the morning. We have only one camel—the old
female—to carry our belongings.

I lie awake for a long time, not thinking, trying to feel—
testing for sadness, anger, anything, but I am as empty as
the clay cups after the dancing. When I sleep finally, it's
a long, dreamless sleep. In the morning Dadi shakes me

awake gently. The sun is fully up, and he helps me to sit. He drops something warm and heavy into my lap. It takes a moment for my head to clear.

A puppy with a large, round belly and soft brown fur picks at my fingers with sharp teeth. I look up, and Dadi is smiling. I hand the wriggling thing back to him.

"We'd better tie him up in a basket," I say.

"Don't you want to carry him?" asks Dadi.

I shrug. I feel exhausted and heavy. The thought of walking through the desert all day defeats me before I'm even out from under my quilt. I'll be lucky if I can carry myself.

I go to the canal and splash water on my face. When I come back, Dadi has loaded the camel with everything but the teapot. The puppy barks a high yap from a basket that hangs next to the water jars on the camel's hump. Dadi hands me a cup of tea and a *chapati*. I haven't eaten since yesterday and am hungry.

"Do you want to ride?" Dadi asks. I decide to walk.

The day passes in a long, monotonous shuffle. Both of us walk in silence. The puppy quiets. Lulled by the stride of the old female camel, he falls asleep on the straw Dadi has laid on the bottom of the basket. His wet, black nose is pressed against an opening between the reeds.

We walk along the riverbed. My feet stumble and slide over the round stones. Dadi picks me up and carries me for a while on his shoulders.

We turn away from the river and follow the railway.

Every two hours a train whistles by, moving fast downhill toward Jacobabad.

It's getting dark when we see Dingra ahead, a tiny settlement around the train stop.

"Do you want to stop here for the night?" asks Dadi.

I shake my head.

"We don't want to walk into the tribal area after dark," he says.

But the moon is up before the sun sets, and we walk far into the night, keeping the road on one side and the train tracks on the other. We stop just short of Bellpat, where tomorrow we leave the road behind and walk along a desert track into the land of the Bugtis.

Over the next two days, we pass through the tribal area without incident. Dadi insists I ride so people will see we're a simple family coming from Sibi to cross the desert. He has left several thousand rupees in his belt, enough to satisfy any thief we should meet. The rest of the notes are rolled into the hollowed wood of the camel saddle frame.

Spring comes early to Cholistan, and already the days are hot. The puppy is panting in his basket. I dip my cup into the water jar and offer him a drink. He tries to wriggle out of the basket and looks at me with bright black eyes. He hasn't had attention since we left, so I pull him out and hold him in my lap for a while. He bites at my fingers. I tap his nose, and he stops biting and looks up at me. He's a smart one. Instead he licks my palm. I tap his nose again, and he looks at me as if to ask "Now what?" He drinks more water and falls asleep in the crook of my arm. I put him back in the basket. He barks for a long while before falling asleep again.

Our trip passes in a dull routine of walking, sometimes riding the old female camel, and stopping to eat and sleep.

Dadi has given up trying to talk to me. He walks along, singing in his husky voice, and sometimes talks to the camel, sometimes to the puppy. He calls the puppy *Sher Dil*, which means "lion heart." It's a good name, for the puppy is strong and unafraid. When Dadi lets him out of his basket at night, he tumbles and tugs at the edge of our quilts and runs in circles before collapsing between us.

I have thought about Guluband often since we left Sibi. I summon his image and want to feel sad or angry or lonely. But apart from moments at night when I sit up in stark fear, waking from a dream of guns raining bullets down on him, I feel strangely detached, as if he's with a part of me that now is gone. The only feeling I have left is of weight and heat and the white dusty air as we walk through the desert on the alien side of the Indus River.

On the eighth night we reach Rahimyar Khan. We must finish shopping for Phulan's wedding. Since we have just the one camel, we go straight into the bazaar. It's strange to see so many people after a week alone in the desert.

In the bazaar, Dadi leaves me to look for shawls for Phulan's dowry, while he goes off to find Uncle and a place to tie the camel. I finger the prickly polyester and wool shawls arranged in bright stacks of red, green, turquoise, and yellow, folded to show clumsy stitching. I don't like any of them. The shopkeeper thinks I'm a child and tells me outrageous prices.

I leave the shop and walk down the crowded lane to another, where an old man who reminds me of Grandfather sits peacefully on his floor, staring out into the daylight. He starts when he sees me, staring as if he's seen a ghost.

"I'm looking for fine shawls for my sister Phulan's dowry," I announce. The old man invites me inside.

"What color?" he asks. I rub one bare foot over the other, thinking about it.

"Well, what color are her eyes?" asks the old man, his eyes surrounded by skin crinkled with kindness.

I haven't thought of it, but Phulan's eyes are a tawny color like liquid gold. I try to explain, and he lays a finger against his lips, thinking a moment.

"Wait here, child," he says, and jumps down from the platform of his shop floor, slips into his sandals, and disappears around the corner.

I walk through the shop, looking at the woolen shawls stacked neatly, the soft colors mixed together unlike in the other shops. I see a pale green the color of desert shrubs and pull a woolen shawl from the pile. As I hold it up and the folds shake out, my breath catches. The embroidery at the ends is like the flowers on the trellises in the landowners' gardens—deep, dark red like desert roses, and delicate pink like the blossoms of *kharin*.

The *kharin* should be blooming when we reach Cholistan, and for the first time since Wardak led Guluband away, I feel a stirring in the place I'd thought my heart had left.

When the old man returns, he has a packet wrapped in crumpled yellow newspaper under one arm, a stack of pale-colored shawls under the other.

"How much is this one?" I ask, holding out the soft green one.

"It's very expensive," he says. "It's *pashmina* from Kashmir. It was made for my mother before her wedding."

"How expensive?" I ask impatiently. I want this for Phulan. It will be beautiful with her tiger eyes.

He looks at my desert nomad's clothes, the glass bangles on my arm, and the tribal silver bracelet on one ankle above my rough bare feet.

"Eight thousand rupees," he says.

My jaw drops. My ears burn with shame, and I turn to walk out of his shop.

"Wait," says the man. "What's your name, child?"

"Shabanu."

A smile starts slowly at the corners of his mouth and grows until it lights up his entire brown face.

"It's the name of a princess," I say, lifting my chin and looking him in the eye.

"It also was the name of my mother," he says, and unties the packet of yellowed newspaper.

His hands are gnarled and his beard wispy. He folds back the last piece of paper and pulls out an exquisite gray-colored piece of cloth as light as a spider's web.

"My father gave this *shatoosh* to my mother," he says. "Would you like it?"

Pale pink and green embroidery so fine I can't see the stitches curls along the edges of the gossamer shawl. It is the most beautiful thing I have ever seen or touched.

"I could never afford this," I whisper.

"Nor could I. They don't make *shatoosh* anymore. There are so few wild goats, and nobody has the patience to gather the chin hairs from the bushes where they graze. So even the richest man in Pakistan can't afford to buy a *shatoosh*. There are no more."

"But you could sell it for a fortune!"

"If I can't buy a *shatoosh,* how can I sell one?" he asks. "My wife is dead and I have no children. My mother visits me in dreams to ask what I've done with her *shatoosh*. I was ashamed to tell her it lies wrapped in newspaper under my bed. I've been looking for someone to give it to. I believe I have found the right person."

"But my sister Phulan . . ."

"Ah, Phulan of the tawny eyes," he says, resting his finger against his lips again. He turns to the stack he's carried with him and sets them out between us on a clean but worn cloth.

They are dull colors, and I protest that Phulan likes brightness. As he unfolds each one I feel the wool. It's so soft and the embroidery so exquisite, I want them all.

"When Phulan is grown, she'll dress in bright colors," says the shopkeeper. "She needs a white shawl to cover her bright dresses for special occasions and a fawn shawl to keep her warm in the day, so the gold in her eyes will show."

I know he's right, and we sit down to choose which is better embroidery, which is the finer weave, the better color for Phulan's eyes. When Dadi finds me, we have settled on the white and fawn shawls. While Dadi and the shopkeeper talk about prices, I return to finger the pale green *pashmina*.

"This is my wedding present for Phulan," says the shopkeeper, handing it to me. "May she have many sons."

As we leave I try to think of a special way to thank him, to tell him I've always dreamed of having a *shatoosh* but never imagined I would.

"Thank you," I say. It comes out in a whisper. The shopkeeper puts his hand on my shoulder and looks at Dadi.

"She really is a princess, your Shabanu," he says.

I wonder if God has sent this man to show me I still have a heart, after all.

We go next to the gold bazaar, where Dadi buys earrings for Phulan and a necklace for Mama, who has never owned gold.

By the time we leave Rahimyar Khan, the camel is loaded with brass pots for Auntie and other gifts from Uncle, so Dadi and I will have to walk most of the next four days until we reach home.

We enter the Cholistan Desert as soon as we leave the edge of the city. The heat shimmers from the ground shortly after Dadi and I set off at sunrise.

"Are you sorry you have only daughters?" I ask. Dadi has been silent for some time.

"God has been very good to us, and I'm not sorry about anything." Dadi leads the camel, and I walk beside him, swinging my arms, listening to the tinkle of my glass bangles. I've learned to keep the *chadr* in place, and even to like the way it blows out behind me as I walk. I'll never wrap it around me like a shroud, the way Phulan does.

We stop to rest under a stand of thorn trees, and Dadi sits on a branch that runs along the ground. He unwinds his turban, and I notice the lines around the corners of his mouth and eyes.

I feel better, and while the camel kneels, eating in the shade, I take the puppy out of his basket so he can relieve himself. I walk to the other side of the camel to take out *chapati*s and tea. Sher Dil pounces on the corner of my *chadr,* yanking my head back and landing me on my backside in the sand.

Dadi throws his head back and laughs as I haven't heard him laugh since we left Cholistan. I try to be dignified, but Sher Dil leaps on me as if I were another puppy. I laugh too.

That night I wrap the *shatoosh* around me. For all its lightness, it's warm as my quilt. I look up at the stars and am surprised at how brightly they pulse. I haven't noticed them in a while.

I scatter pieces of onion around us on the ground. Sher Dil climbs under the quilt. As I fall asleep I hear the ancient symphony of the animals coming to the nearby *toba* to drink, the gong and plunk of their large brass bells muffled by the dunes.

Cholistan, I am home!

Dowry

Phulan and Mama come running to meet us, their *chadr*s flying out behind them when we are still half a mile from home. Loping along behind is Mithoo, bigger by a head than he was when we left, his legs still too long and flying out in funny little kicks. Tears spring to my eyes, and I run, arms wide, to Mama and embrace her fiercely.

Dadi joins us and we walk toward our hut, all talking at once.

77

"We have dozens of new baby camels," says Phulan, who wears a red *chadr* over her hair, her face lovely and golden in the full sun. I'm so pleased she has shed her pretensions and her black *chadr* that I hardly mind her insinuating she's been looking after my job.

As we near the huts Auntie waddles out, puffing noisily, my two cousins in tow. They've grown too.

"Are these my pots?" asks Auntie, thumping the shining brass with her knuckles.

"They're good, heavy ones," says Mama. "They'll last longer than you will." We use only clay pots.

Auntie sniffs and inspects the rest of our cargo to see what else Uncle has sent from Rahimyar Khan.

Sher Dil announces his presence with a loud "Yap! yap!" Auntie leaps backward and pulls her *chadr* over her nose. Phulan and I try not to laugh, but Phulan has to turn her head away.

Mama reaches up and unlashes the basket, and my cousins jump up and down, squealing and clapping their hands. Sher Dil pushes the lid aside with his wet, black nose, blinks once, and recognizes the boys as what he's been looking for: puppies to play with. They chase one another, and Sher Dil takes turns jumping on each cousin, licking their faces and barking with joy to be out of the basket. The boys turn him over to inspect him and rub his round belly. Sher Dil paws the air, whining happily.

"We'll have to keep our eye on him every second when we get to the settled area," Mama says. She had been fond of the dog that was poisoned last year.

Dowry

We unload the camel, and I carry our cooking pots through the neatly swept courtyard. The curved mud walls and spiky thatch of the hut are welcoming, but I feel like a stranger. I stoop to enter, and it takes a moment for my eyes to adjust. Metal cups and serving platters stand in neat, shiny rows against the wall. The reed mats feel fresh and smooth underfoot. A baby goat is tethered to a stick along one side, a stack of bright quilts just out of reach. And the large metal trunk for Phulan's dowry takes up a great deal of space—everything as before.

I step back out into the courtyard to fetch more of our gear. In the shade of the mud mound where we keep milk and wheat flour, Grandfather sits, shading his eyes with one gnarled hand. I think for a moment he doesn't recognize me.

"Shabanu?" he says, a long-toothed smile spreading under his white mustache. "You've grown a foot!"

I bend to kiss his hand, and he pulls me down beside him.

"Tell me, what did you see at Sibi?" This is the old Grandfather, back again after periods of frailty and seeming distant. Sometimes I worry that we'll never see the old Grandfather again before he dies.

Phulan looks over her shoulder as she carries my quilt inside, but she says nothing and returns to help carry sacks of flour and lentils from the camel.

I tell Grandfather about seeing Derawar and thinking of him there, and about the Bugtis, the carnival, the Afghan Wardak, the celebration, the trip back, the re-

79

markable man in the bazaar at Rahimyar Khan, and the *shatoosh*. I talk quickly, with animation, the words tumbling out faster and faster, until I am breathless and have nothing left to tell. He covers my hand with his to make me be quiet and tilts my chin up so I'm looking into his kind, old eyes.

"We are proud people, and there is nothing that gives so much pride as our animals. You can grieve for your Guluband—he was the finest we've had."

The tears come slowly, leaking out over my cheeks, down my chin and neck. I weep quietly, Grandfather patting my hand the whole time. I lower my head onto my arms, folded over my knees, and rock back and forth, the grief spilling out.

Phulan drops a load of camel blankets in the middle of the courtyard and runs to put her arms around me.

"Shh, shh, shh, Shabanu," she croons, as Mama had sung when I was a baby.

Mama brings me a cup of tea, and this time the salty-sweet liquid is a comfort. Dadi joins us, and we talk of Guluband and how we'll miss him, everyone being very kind and acknowledging that in truth he'd been my own camel. Gradually the yapping of Sher Dil and the boys' laughter from outside penetrate the courtyard, and I feel less like a stranger, but still as though I've returned after a long time.

"Come, let's go see the new babies before it gets dark," says Phulan, standing and tugging at my hand.

Dowry

The mothers and babies gather at the *toba* for protection from the night. Their bells ring a fluid melody as natural to the desert as the wind. Mithoo follows, nuzzling me as we walk. I put my arm around his neck. He is growing strong and fine.

As we cross over the last dune to the *toba*, I'm alarmed at how much water has disappeared: it's half full. Along its edge spiky *kharin*, brilliant green sticks joined end-to-end at odd angles, are covered with yellow and pink flowers that look like small dragon faces. Their smell is sweet as desert honey.

I count the babies, twenty-two in all. Most of the females have given birth. In view of Tipu's amorous activities, probably half will drop calves again next year. Most of the little ones nurse, flicking their tails.

Phulan has brought a goatskin bag she has made to feed Mithoo. She loosens the mesh sack that covers the udder of a weaning mother. I keep her yearling offspring away while Phulan draws milk into the feeding bag. The udder is small, the milk drying up. When she finishes I let the yearling go, and he nearly knocks Phulan over to get to his mother's teat.

Mithoo bucks and grunts, and I feel a little jealous when he gambols after Phulan, who takes his bag to tie to a branch of the thorn tree.

"He's so tall I can't hold my arms high enough," Phulan explains. "I'm happy you're back. My ribs are bruised from this one poking me while I try to feed him," she says, nudging Mithoo away with her knee. I grab his straining neck while Phulan finishes tying the goatskin to the branch. She unwinds the cord tied around one corner.

As she steps aside, Mithoo takes a sideways lunge, and has his nimble lips around the Phulan-made nipple before a single drop can fall to the ground. We laugh as he grunts, butting the bag with his forehead.

A soft pain jolts beneath my ribs as I watch Mithoo nurse, and I think my heart is beginning to mend.

We return at dusk to find Auntie has slaughtered a goat to celebrate our return. Dadi skins it for her, the boys standing by, their eyes hungry. Mama cuts the meat into cubes to be roasted on the fire. It's nearly dark, and my stomach is grumbling. It'll be a while before the meat is ready.

While it's cooking, Dadi and I unwrap the shawls and the gold. Phulan's eyes are wide and she exclaims softly as Dadi folds back the paper from each piece.

Mama bites her lower lip when Dadi fastens the new gold necklace around her neck. He takes out his snuff-box with the mirror on the lid so she can admire the way it nestles in the hollow of her brown throat.

Auntie sits at the edge of the fire circle, watching quietly. Even she gasps when Dadi holds up Phulan's nose ring. The fire gleams off the golden circle and glows in the tiny rubies that dangle from its edge. We are struck silent, and concern for the cost of what we've bought creases Mama's brow.

Dadi looks from face to face, disappointed at the silence.

"We're rich now," he tells us, and stands up to dance around the fire. Phulan joins him, clapping out a rhythm, her new gold bangles jangling on her arm. Mama clicks her tongue, and Auntie picks up the nose ring to inspect it. Nobody in our family has ever had such a dowry.

"Come on," says Dadi, lifting Mama to her feet. Even Auntie claps her hands and we all give thanks, singing and kicking up clouds of dust as we dance around the fire in our bare feet.

Phulan and Mama leave us and sit down again to go through Phulan's new jewelry and clothes. They pack them away while Auntie and I make *chapati*s and take the meat from the fire.

The meat is yeasty and smooth. We eat until we can eat no more, and Dadi tells Mama stories of our trip. She listens with a faraway look in her eyes, visiting where we've been through his remembering.

Grandfather snores beside Phulan's trunk, and the boys sprawl, Sher Dil between them, on the mats. Auntie and Phulan pick them up and carry them across the courtyard. Auntie shoos Sher Dil out with her broom.

Phulan and I try to wake Grandfather, but he is sleeping too soundly, so we cover him with his quilt. From the looks Mama and Dadi gave each other over the fire, we know they want to be alone, and we share Grandfather's twine-strung bed in the courtyard under the stars.

Nose Pegs

The sky is pearl-gray when I awake, Mithoo's nose within an inch of mine. I reach up and rub his forehead. He snorts, and Phulan grabs the quilt away and pushes me out of bed.

Yawning and rubbing my eyes, I tie a piece of soap into the corner of my *chadr*. I pick up two earthen pots and a padded ring to balance one pot on my head. The other fits under my arm, balanced on my hip. Mithoo and I set off for the *toba*.

Mithoo's small brass bell jingles cheerfully as he bobs his head, impatient for me to fold back the reed door leading outside from the courtyard. The red cord holding his bell is too tight for his thickening neck, and I promise him a new one. Sher Dil squeezes through the door as I fasten it shut again.

Crossing the dunes to the *toba*, I think of Guluband. He seems a part of my life that is long past. His going has taught me both the strength of my will and its limits. I know Dadi thinks my bent for freedom is dangerous, and I'm learning to save my spirit for when it can be useful.

With Guluband, Tipu, and Kalu gone, Dadi will have to train several of the three-year-old camels to work. I make Mithoo carry the empty goatskin to the *toba*.

I look out over our dwindling water supply. Lavender ribbons reflect from the sky in the last few moments before the sun rises. We probably have a month, perhaps three weeks, before the water disappears into the air. The monsoon begins in two months—the time for flowers, mushrooms, and weddings.

Two-toed camel footprints are baked into the shiny clay at the outer edges of the *toba*. I lift my skirt with one hand, and the mud squirts between my toes as I enter the water. I push aside the green scum that floats just under the surface and drape the edge of my *chadr* over the mouth of the pot as a filter.

I take the filled pot to the bathing rock at the edge of the *toba* and lift my tunic over my head. I throw my hair forward and pour water on it.

The sun edges over the horizon. I can feel its heat on my back and shoulders as the water trickles over my scalp. I rub the loamy soap into my hair. I squeeze my eyes shut, letting the soapy water drain down over my shoulders and neck, rubbing it into my skin before rinsing off to conserve every drop. Mama bathed Phulan and me with a single cup of water when we were small.

My fingers touch a sore spot on my chest, and I look to see if there is a bruise. My shoulders are drawn forward with the chill of the water, and at first I don't notice that the skin around my breasts has begun to swell. I throw my shoulders back and stare in disbelief.

I explore my sore little breast buds with mixed feelings. Phulan's breasts have been increasing in size for more than a year. I wonder with a vague longing whether I'll ever be as beautiful as Phulan.

On the other embankment, poor Mithoo walks slowly, skirting the herd, his head turned away from me, bobbing and still looking for a nursing female that will take him to her.

I look up as Phulan crosses the last dune to the *toba*. The sun shines through her red *chadr*, outlining her slender figure in its glow. Two pots balance on her head, and she walks with the liquid grace of a desert woman. She wrinkles her nose when she sees me watching. I hope there's no trace of envy in my eyes. She dips a knee for me to lift off the pots.

"Auntie came out and shook me awake just a second after you left. She can't stand for me to be comfortable." She pushes out her lower lip, and her eyes flash sideways.

I press the damp soap into her hand.

"Here," I say. "A bath will make you feel good."

"Stay with me," she says. "I want to know everything that happened at Sibi."

It's been two years since Phulan has been to the fair. She always says she doesn't want to go, that it's for little girls. I thought she was being spiteful, that deep down she really wanted to go. But I no longer care about going again.

I hug her and tell her I'll wash her hair. She pulls her tunic over her head. Her breasts have grown to the size of apples! The vague new longing washes over me again.

As I soap her hair I tell her about the Bugti girl and her lover. Phulan gasps, throws back her hair, and blots the soap from her eyes with the edge of her *chadr*.

"Would they really kill her? Couldn't she get away?" Her eyes are wide with horror.

"Where is there to hide in the desert? I'm sure they found her and killed her. Both of them."

Phulan shivers and bends her head over the water again. We are silent for a moment.

I tell her about the *shatoosh,* the *paan* maker, and the big wheel. It sounds juvenile to me now, and I feel awkward. I look at my sturdy hands as they rub soap into her hair. Her fingers curve gracefully around the edge of the rock.

She tells me Auntie has grown more tyrannical by the day. Even the prospect of Uncle's visit next month—and his gifts of perfume and new dresses—fails to improve her spirits.

"She's jealous because she's old and fat, and you're the center of attention with the wedding so near."

Poor Auntie. Her father was rich. But she was fat and he couldn't find her a husband. Uncle was a hardworking, decent man with a job in the city. That's how marriages are made. It was a good match for both of them, for different reasons.

After breakfast Dadi comes out of the house with a leather bag and a coil of rope.

"We have to peg noses today," he says. When Uncle was here this winter, he and Dadi pegged the noses of four three-year-olds to train for work. Even with an extra man, we'd had a difficult time.

Phulan's eyes widen and she pulls her *chadr* across her nose.

"Don't be such a goose," I tell her. Auntie also looks apprehensive as we walk back toward the *toba*.

Dadi, Grandfather, and I talk gently to the young camels, trying to get a hand on one. They trot around, showing the whites of their eyes. Their behavior is silly. We never beat our camels, and they have no reason to fear us. I hold out my hand, palm skyward with a piece of brown sugar on it.

My target is Xhush Dil, which means "happy heart." He is large-boned and playful. He can't resist sugar. Grandfather strokes Xhush Dil's neck while Dadi ties a loop of rope around his foreleg. Making a figure eight, he hobbles the camel's leg. While Mama feeds Xhush Dil another lump of sugar, Dadi and I tie his opposite rear leg, and with a mighty tug we pull his legs out from under him. He grunts as he hits the ground.

Dadi grabs Xhush Dil's upper lip, and Auntie holds on to Dadi's waist while Mama pierces the camel's nose with a long needle. Xhush Dil is still trying to get his lip from Dadi's grasp to find more brown sugar. At first he doesn't realize what's happened. After withdrawing the needle, Mama puts the pointed end of the wooden peg into the hole and forces it through. She attaches a goathair cord to the peg in one swift move, just as Xhush Dil jerks his head away.

The camel roars in surprise and pain and thrashes his head from side to side, sending Dadi and Auntie flying. They land in a heap on the ground. Phulan has stood the whole time behind Mama, her hand clasped daintily over her mouth. Her eyes are laughing as Auntie struggles like an overturned turtle, but she hurries to help her up.

Dadi unties the hobbles, and Xhush Dil lurches to his feet. His eyes slide wildly from side to side and he snorts and grunts. Dadi keeps a gentle hand on the reins, and

Xhush Dil feels the pressure on his smarting nose. When he is calmer, Mama puts mint water on it and he roars again, tossing his head, but now it's more for show. Grandfather quiets him with a soft clucking sound.

The sun is extremely hot now, and we spend the afternoon sleeping under a tarpaulin tied from the doorway to the courtyard wall to catch the breeze.

Over the next week we watch our water dwindle. In the heat of the afternoons, before the wind and dust kick up, we work on Phulan's dowry, adjusting everything to fit.

We also dry herbs and think about prepartions for leaving the *toba* as the water slips away with the hot desert wind.

Channan Pir

Our thoughts turn to Channan Pir, the desert shrine where women pray for sons and good marriages for their daughters. Travelers stop to tell us a caravan of women will pass on their way to the shrine in a week.

We leave the night of the next full moon. Grandfather is in fine form. He and Sher Dil gather the camels and our few sheep. Grandfather sings the whole time, his voice strong. The animals follow its sound through the dunes, their bells tinkling.

Phulan and I ride in a mirrored pannier on Xhush Dil's back. Mama and Auntie ride another camel. The animals are dressed in wedding livery, their harnesses festooned with silver medallions and bright silk tassels, with shells, bells, and mirrors sewn along the edges of the saddle blankets. Above their knees the camels wear woven goathair bracelets with beaded fringes.

Dadi, Grandfather, and the little boys ride with us for a while. Sher Dil trots back and forth, guarding the ewes, lambs, and baby camels. He is still a pup, but his shoulders are growing strong, his chest deep and powerful, his fur glossy.

Phulan looks regal with the red *chadr* over her shiny black hair. She looks like a flower blooming in the desert sunset, the wind whipping her clothes around her in sheets of color.

Mama too is dressed in silk, a sequined and embroidered turquoise tunic that shows the green flecks in her mysterious dark eyes. Her teeth and nose disk flash as she tosses her head, and I wish I were half as graceful as she and Phulan are.

Auntie wears an emerald silk tunic and skirt. It is plain, and I pity her that nothing she wears can show her good points, which sometimes are hidden even from our hearts.

I ride beside Phulan among the tasseled cushions in the pannier. The camels pitch us forward and side to side.

Grandfather reminds me to pray for the soul of Grandmother, who died when Dadi was a boy.

"She was beautiful," he says, his eyes far off on the distant dunes. "She was so proud when I rode off on Kalu, although she also was fearful."

"What did you wear, Grandfather?" I ask.

"We wore starched khaki tunics and billowing trousers, a fez, and a silver sword."

Grandfather touches the bundle that contains his papers, fez, sword, and other things from the past.

"*Hunteray,* Kalu," he says to the old female camel he rides. Grandfather calls all camels Kalu after the great black martial beast he rode in battle for the nawab's army.

We travel along the clay track that used to be the ancient Hakra River bed.

"I remember," says Grandfather, his eyes far away again, "sitting as a boy under the great banyan tree at the edge of the river, dreaming of when I could fight for the Abassi prince."

Auntie rolls her eyes. Phulan and I look at each other. Grandfather's mind travels back and forth in time with amazing ease. He relives history as if he had been there, regardless of the century. The Hakra River dried up three thousand years ago.

He turns to Mama. "I remember when the Rajput prince brought your people from India to build the fort at Derawar. They're Hindus."

"But Grandfather," she says gently, "we converted to Islam when Akbar came, four hundred years ago."

"Yes, yes," says Grandfather, brushing her protest aside. "The Hindu Raja of Bikaner had seized all of Cholistan from Qutb-ud-din, the Abassi general. But we fought valiantly.

"Both sides had elephants. The elephants lined up on either side of the fortress walls and intertwined their trunks. Lances and spears fell from their sides as if they wore armor. We drove the raja back to India and built fort doors higher than trees, with sword blades at the top so his elephants couldn't knock them down. But the camels saved the day!"

We ride in silence for a time, and Grandfather nods off.

"*Allah-o-Akbar!*" he shouts, sitting straight so suddenly it knocks his turban askew.

"It was that battle! We pursued the infantry. The artillery was behind the dunes in the high desert. They fixed their cannons on us and a full-load shot hit Kalu in the chest."

Grandfather is silent for a second, his head straight and proud.

"Kalu charged another furlong before he fell." Grandfather has walked with a stick and a limp ever since.

"Father," says Dadi. "That was the battle Pakistan fought with India over Kutch after independence." Grandfather's confusion doesn't matter. He and Kalu had been a brave pair, and his stories always thrill us.

Grandfather nods off again, and we travel in silence until the evening breeze picks up and we see the dust from the women's caravan ahead.

As our camels pull away from Dadi and the herd to join the caravan, Mithoo tries to follow us. But Sher Dil runs after him, barking fiercely and nipping at his legs. My poor motherless Mithoo shifts direction to rejoin the herd. He dips his head and turns it back over his shoulder, his eyes still on us.

So much is changing, and I've only just noticed. Like a breeze gathering strength, all of us—animals and humans—are growing up.

The camels know the track to Channan Pir well and need no guidance. Every year we make the trek to the shrine to ask for some kindness from the saint who is protector of all children.

It will be another hour before the moon is up, about the same time we should catch up with the caravan. We listen to the bells of our herd until they are swallowed by the night.

The sky is already bright with stars. Phulan and I lie back and count the long, bright arcs they make when they fall. A rim of moon slips up over a mound of sand, and its blue-white light washes over the desert. Suddenly the sand, which looks slatternly gray in the sunlight, shimmers like an ocean of diamonds.

Before the moon is fully clear of the dunes, we hear the singing of the women in the caravan ahead. Without warning, Xhush Dil's great shaggy head lifts back and his front feet kick out, and we dance in the moonlight. A song rises in my throat, and Phulan lies back against her cushions to listen as I sing about a man whose lover God has taken away and sent to live among the stars where he sees her every night. He can never have her.

The women shout greetings as we draw near. "Ho! You must be looking for husbands and sons!" And there is much laughter. Mama and Auntie have cousins among this festive troupe, but it will be difficult to find them. There are too many camels to count, all decorated with mirrors and bells.

Phulan sleeps. We pass the night in a magical glitter of sand and moonlight, bells and mirrors, singing and clapping and the camaraderie of women.

As we approach Channan Pir the birds are just beginning to twitter in the trees around the shrine. There are more camels as we draw closer. Sleeping women on bright quilts increase in number from a few scattered shapes to a sea of blankets touching edge to edge. We walk the camels directly to the miraculous mound of rocks under which the saint is buried.

We circle the tomb once, passing under the thorn tree that shades the mound and past the eternal lamps beside the grave. Green, red, and blue flags flutter softly against the silvery sky. We pass the old ocher mosque with its three green domes and look for a place to camp and leave the camels.

Mama and Auntie find their cousins and invite them to have tea with us after we have found a spot near theirs.

Phulan builds a fire while Mama and I unload the camels, and Auntie pours water into the kettle. The ground feels shaky under our feet after pitching and rolling in the panniers all night.

I hobble and tether the camels and am about to give them fodder when I hear the unmistakable throaty voice of Sharma, Mama's favorite cousin and my favorite aunt. Mama takes her in her arms and buries her face in Sharma's hair, and they just hold each other and laugh.

Fatima, her daughter, takes Phulan and me by the hand, and we look each other over. Fatima has changed little since we saw her at Adil's wedding last year. She is as delicate and small as her mother is tall and straight. Her face is soft, with a small, round nose, full lips, and tiny, even teeth. Her bosom is full, and although she is not beautiful, she has her mother's warmth and strength.

Auntie doesn't look up from the fire, which she pokes under the kettle. She disapproves of Sharma, who left her husband because he beat her. He was older and already had one wife who had borne him no sons. He married Sharma in the hope she'd bear a boy child. When Fatima was born he began beating both of them, and Sharma refused to lie with him.

Slowly she built her own herd of goats and sheep, as well as her courage. Then she left him. Sharma and Fatima are not afraid to live alone. Anyone who might want to harm Sharma should think twice; she is better able to take care of herself than most men are.

Auntie thinks Fatima is a double disgrace. At sixteen she isn't married, doesn't want to marry, and Sharma has no intention of forcing her to marry.

Sharma is bold and outspoken. Most men don't like her and are afraid of her. Not Dadi. He thinks she's wonderful.

Sharma's hair is streaked with gray, and her skin is dry and creased. But her hands are graceful and long, her breasts high and firm, and her teeth white and straight. She is about Mama's age, perhaps thirty.

When the camels are fed we sit, ankles crossed, eating *chapati*s and drinking tea, catching up on the news; Adil's wife is expecting a baby in three months; his elder brother has just had a second child, a girl—too bad, it seems to run in the family. They laugh and slap their knees. Auntie draws her *chadr* across her face and sits at the edge of the circle.

Well after the sun is up and the heat has gathered, the bagpipes and drums begin. Sharma and Fatima promise to have supper with us so we can talk into the night. It's so rare to see relatives, we never run out of things to say.

We put our belongings away and head toward the shrine to pray for sons for Phulan. We cover our heads and gather our *chadr*s in folds around our shoulders. We walk silently and are caught in the crush of women sitting with baskets before them heaped with flowers and lumps of white sugar candy. The garlands sell for twenty rupees apiece. Each of us buys a garland for Phulan.

We approach the peeling ocher mosque in our bare feet. Auntie's feet are tender from wearing leather shoes, and she sucks air in through her crooked brown teeth as her soles touch the hot sand.

Women kneel in rows in the packed mud courtyard of the mosque. Rotating their bodies, they toss their oiled hair over their heads, back and forth and around and around with a whipping motion like horses' tails, in a frenzy of devotion.

Women whirl like dervishes, ankle bracelets jangling, their skirts flying out like disks of color. All around are women: wailing women, silent women with children clinging to their skirts, women dancing and playing flutes and singing songs about the life of the Channan Pir. Beside the entrance to the shrine a woman, her head thrown back, wails her anguish at having lost a child. Another sits in a trance, a small girl crawling under her knees.

The queue grows quieter as we approach the mound of stones. Colored flags snap and curl in the breeze. I lay a fistful of sweets and my garland beside the tomb and bow my head amid buzzing flies. I close my eyes, and the combined sweetness of crushed flowers and burning incense makes me dizzy. I pray with all my heart that Phulan will have sons. In the second before someone shoves me aside to make room for another supplicant, I pray she and Hamir will be happy, and that life will not be too difficult for her.

Afterward, we push our way back to our camp. The camels lie with their legs under them, dozing in the sun. Flies collect in the corners of their eyes, and the heat presses down on us so we can barely breathe. Mama and I tip the panniers on their sides and tie *chadr*s at their corners, making a shelter against the sun. We have a cup of water, then lie down on our quilts to sleep through the burning white afternoon.

Before the sun sets I take Xhush Dil out into the desert to collect fodder and firewood. We haven't gone far when we hear bagpipes and drums from the camps where the men wait for their women. A roar goes up, and Xhush Dil and I move closer to see. We stop under a thorn tree. If Dadi sees me he'll be angry. Xhush Dil lifts his head to nibble the leaves overhead, and I stand behind his hump, holding on to the tree trunk with one arm.

The men stand several deep, jostling for position. One sweeps clear a circle, dust rising in gray clouds around him. Two men wearing nothing but loincloths stand outside the circle, flexing their legs and arms. I am too far away to see their faces clearly.

The crowd cheers as one of the bare-chested men, with shoulders broad as an ox yoke and a round, hard belly, pushes through the circle and lifts his arms above his bald head. But a roar of approval goes up as the other man, much smaller than the first, with a handsome black mustache, comes into the ring, his broad back glistening in the lowering sun.

The two crouch and circle each other, and the tempo of the drums and bagpipes quickens. The smaller man, clearly the crowd's favorite, turns toward me, thick muscles bunching in his thighs and calves. Something is oddly familiar about him. The larger man lunges, the smaller dodges, catching the arm of the other as he hurtles past, levering the immense weight and hurling him onto his back in the dust.

They remind me of Kalu and Tipu. . . . All at once I realize it's Dadi! My heart thunders. I want to ride through the circle of wildly cheering men and make them stop.

But I am stuck to the tree as if it's caught me with its thorns. The huge man regains his feet and, in so doing, pulls Dadi's leg out from under him, slamming him to the ground. The large man pounces on top of Dadi, who rolls away an instant before the other smashes to the earth.

Again Dadi uses the momentum of the other man's lunge to flip him onto his back and pin his shoulders to the ground. It's over in less than a minute, and Dadi, the favorite, has won. The crowd is nearly mad with ecstasy, calling for blood.

My heart thrashes inside my ribs as I yank Xhush Dil's head down from the thorn branches and turn him. The motion catches Dadi's eye, and my last glimpse of him is of a heaving chest and angry eyes.

We dash up the great, soft dunes and down the other side, over the hot white desert, the wind stinging my face through tears. The sun is gone, and I have little light to gather wood. But I do it with a fury and return with bulging bags to the happy warmth of the women.

As Phulan fills the kettle, Mama begins slapping dough into *chapatis*. She smiles as she works, looking forward to Sharma and Fatima's visit. I stare at her and wonder, How can she stand him? How can she let a man who would fight another naked man touch her . . . and do what the camels do?

"What is it, Shabanu?" she asks, the smile still hovering on her mouth. I turn away, and she goes back to her bowl.

Sharma

We hear Sharma's deep, husky voice laughing and talking, calling out to women camped around us and moving animals from her path long before we see her.

Fatima carries a steaming pot of spiced lentils, and Mama gives each of them a dress she's sewn. Fatima holds hers before her lovely bosom, and Phulan nudges me with her elbow.

Sharma takes over making *chapati*s, and Mama whisks

milk and sugar into the tea, and they talk about the preparations for Phulan's wedding. Sharma will bring her *jelabi-wallah*, who fries crispy, sugar-filled pretzels in pink oil. Fatima has a friend who sells flowers; she will bring tuberoses, with the fragrance of royal weddings. Phulan's eyes glisten, and her sculpted fingers clasp and unclasp with pleasure.

I say little and try hard not to stare at Fatima. How I long to be like her—never to marry, to stay in the warm, safe circle of women.

After we've eaten and the stars are brilliant and Mama has shown Sharma and Fatima all of Phulan's dowry, as well as my *shatoosh*, they sit back and Sharma tells a story about a woman, her friend, who was stoned to death because her husband accused her of looking at another man.

Mama urges me to tell about the Bugti girl and her lover. They listen, horrified and delighted by the stories. Panic rises in my chest, tears building pressure behind my eyes.

Sharma takes me by the wrist and pulls me toward her, encircling me in her arms like a small child.

"Don't be frightened, Shabanu," she whispers against my ear. "There are evil men in the world, but the love of a good man is the most beautiful thing God can give us."

How can she say that after what she's been through with her terrible husband? She laughs her rich, deep laugh.

I think of Murad, his gentle eyes and his fairness at games. Is any man a good man? In a year I shall be married to him. If he isn't a good man, I shall be like Sharma—strong and independent.

Still holding me, Sharma sings a song, a *ghazal* about a desert man who searches for his love in the desert as if she were water. Fatima brings her lute, and we listen to their rich, dark voices intertwine with the delicate sounds of the strings.

Sharma sings as if she is in a trance, and when she has sung two or three *ghazal*s, she announces that she will sing a *kafi*, a poetic song about the Channan Pir.

Jalal-ud-din Sukh Bokhari stood on the riverside,
A Muslim son to the raja he truly prophesied

sings Sharma, her clean, husky voice traveling back four centuries, quietly setting the story at Uch Sharif, on the banks of the river that has wandered away, leaving this place a desert.

The story is of Raja Sher Shah, the Rajput prince of Bikaner, who hears Bokhari's prophecy that a child conceived by one of his wives, a Muslim, will grow up to be a Muslim saint.

Sharma's voice rises and falls in trills and cadences as the story unfolds, and a crowd of women gathers outside the circle of our fire. They bring more wood, their shawls, and quilts and quietly make room for more women.

When he learned of the birth, the Hindu raja took the infant out into the desert and threw him onto a mound of dirt, leaving him to die in the wilderness.

Here Sharma pauses to catch her breath, and Fatima's tiny fingers pluck out the lilting music on her lute, the

105

crowd saying "Va, va, va," softly expressing their pleasure.

The raja cast the infant out into the wild,
He left him on a desert mound
Where thorns and rocks were piled

sings Sharma. But a magnificent cradle carved of fragrant sandalwood descended from heaven, hovered over the mound of earth, and caught the infant. The raja ordered his soldiers to kill the child, but the cradle carried him up into heaven.

When the raja and his men finally went away, the cradle descended again, and the child grew up in the wilderness, protected by the animals of the desert.

The raja became obsessed with killing the child and frequently sent his soldiers out to search for him, but the animals would warn the boy, and the sandalwood cradle would lift him from danger. The child grew into a wise and gentle man, beloved of all people of the desert, Hindu and Muslim both.

Because of the miracle and the Channan Pir's simplicity and wisdom, the people of the desert became his followers. Many Hindus converted to Islam because of the saint, but Hindus and Muslims alike come to worship at the mound of rocks where the infant was thrown, and where his body lies today.

The second morning we visit the shrine early, before the pushing and shoving, the singing and dancing begin, when the birds are just stirring in the thick, thorny branches of the tree that stands sentinel over Channan Pir's mound of rocks.

Again, like hens laying eggs, we leave our prayers and hopes for Phulan's sons at the head of the shrine.

For the first time, I feel a communion with the saint; his presence is like a soothing hand on my shoulder. Before Auntie nudges me to move along, I pray for wisdom, and my anger with Dadi eases.

I kiss Sharma and Fatima good-bye as the sun rises behind a thin haze that portends a hot day. While Mama, Phulan, and Sharma jabber about who should bring saris and bangles for Hamir's mother, turbans for Hamir and Murad, and more wheat and sugar to Mehrabpur for the wedding, I turn to the business of saddling Xhush Dil. There are no tears, for we shall see them again when the family collects after the fasting month of Ramadan for the wedding in twelve weeks.

Sharma comes around to the side of the camel and catches me in one arm as I lift a quilt onto the mirrored pannier. She spins me away from my task. The way she reads my thoughts takes my breath away.

"Truly, Shabanu," she says, holding my chin in her hand, "a man's love is a blessing. You and Phulan are lucky. Your father is a good man, and he has seen to it that you will marry well."

I can't answer, because a knot of unidentifiable feeling has paralyzed my throat and tongue and brought tears to my eyes.

"God willing, your brain will unscramble itself soon,

and you will know I speak the truth," she says, giving my cheek a painful tweak. I manage a smile and hug her hard.

"If you say so, Auntie Sharma," I whisper into her hair.

I wonder whether Dadi will be cross with me when we meet farther down the track toward home. If only I can keep my feelings under control!

The breeze is hot and dry with the sun still ringed by haze as we set off for home.

Dadi smiles when he sees us. He gives no clue that he saw me at the wrestling yesterday. My cousins are happy to see Auntie, who smiles for the first time in two days as she takes them from Dadi, hauling them down and wiping their faces, clucking as if Dadi has kept them badly.

Auntie takes every opportunity to show Mama how superior she is for having borne Uncle two sons. Mama always takes it in good humor, but I do wonder; if she ever wishes she'd had sons, she never shows it. I notice for the first time a strain about Auntie's eyes and mouth and an extra swelling of her breasts. Perhaps she will bear another son before the year is out.

Mithoo trots up to Xhush Dil's side, looking up to me for a treat. I have nothing to give him, but I slip to the ground and hug his neck, which seems to have grown even thicker in the two days since I saw him last. He prances as if he's too old for such things, his shoulder as high as my head, his feet each bigger than my hand stretched to its broadest. Then he bleats like a lamb and nuzzles my ear. I sympathize, for I too feel like a child struggling to know what it is to be grown.

Desert Storm

By the time we reach the *toba,* Grandfather has fallen back into his torpid state, like a beetle in winter. Dadi worries about him, and Mama makes special efforts to make things that he likes to eat.

"He'll come back," she tells Dadi. "He's been this way for years, and he always comes back. Don't worry." But Dadi continues to worry, stopping by Grandfather on his string cot in the shade of the courtyard wall to interest him in a camel that's fallen ill or a batch of new lambs. Grandfather just nods and sucks at his *hookah*.

The water in the *toba* is slowly drying up, but Dadi says we have enough for the two months before we leave for Mehrabpur to prepare for the wedding.

One night Phulan shakes me awake in the middle of a deep sleep.

"Shabanu!" she shouts from such a great distance I can barely hear her.

She yanks the quilt away, and suddenly my skin is pierced by thousands of needles. The wind is howling around us. I can't see anything when I open my eyes, but I can tell by the sound and feel that it's a monstrous sand-storm, the kind few living things survive without protection. Phulan pulls me by the hand, but I yank away.

"Mithoo!" I stumble about the courtyard, tripping over huddled chickens, clay pots, and bundles of reeds that have broken away from the entrance. "Mithoo!"

Hands outstretched, I feel my way around the court-yard wall, where Mithoo normally sleeps. When I get to where the reeds were stacked on their stalks, lashed side by side and tied to cover the doorway, there is a gaping hole. Quickly I make my way around the courtyard again. Mithoo is gone.

"You can't find him without a light and something to put over your eyes!" Phulan shouts, pulling on my arm. Together we drag the bed through the doorway. Mama struggles to close the window shutters, and Phulan and I manage to push the door shut and wedge the bed against it. Dadi lights a candle and swears softly as the light fills the room. Grandfather and Sher Dil are missing too.

"Where can he have gone?" Mama gasps, her eyes bright with fear. Grandfather had been sound asleep, and the storm must have wakened him.

Dadi uses the candle to light the kerosene storm lantern and pulls the bed away from the door. Mama throws a shawl around his shoulders. He pulls it over his head, and I follow him out to the courtyard, where *khar* shrubs, their shallow roots torn from the dry sand, tumble and hurl themselves against the walls.

With my *chadr* over my face, I can open my eyes enough to see the haze of the lantern in Dadi's hand, the light reflecting from the dust in a tight circle around him.

Auntie has already closed up her house, and Dadi pounds on the door for several minutes before she opens it again and we slip inside.

"Have you seen Grandfather?" asks Dadi.

"And Mithoo and Sher Dil?" I shout.

She stands in the center of her house, mouth open and speechless, her hands raised helplessly. My cousins stand behind her skirt, their eyes wide. From between her feet Sher Dil's black nose glistens in the lamplight. But no Grandfather and no Mithoo.

"Come to our house," Dadi orders her, handing me the lantern. "I'll close up here. Shabanu, come back for me," he says, bending to light Auntie's storm lantern.

When I return, Dadi holds the light so we can see each other.

"Mithoo will be fine," he says, and I know it is a warning not to ask to look for him. "When the wind has died and it's light, we'll find him standing near a tree by the *toba*."

Through my mind race visions of Mithoo trying to stay with the other camels, but the females push him away, as they have since his remarkable birth. They treat him as if he'd been born of another species. Dadi is right. Mithoo has a chance if he can stay with the herd and find shelter in the lee of a dune. But Grandfather can never survive a storm like this.

Dadi holds my hand as we step back into the vicious wind. It slaps us with a terrible force, driving thousands of sand grains through our clothes and against our shielded faces.

"Grandfather! Grandfather!" I shout, but the wind tears the sound from my mouth and hurls it away before I can hear it. I catch wisps of Dadi's voice calling out.

Never have I seen such a storm. I wonder whether Dadi, or even Grandfather, has.

In half an hour we know it's no use. We are exhausted and sick, our skin raw from the sand, our voices gone from shouting and gulping in dust. I close my burning eyes and let Dadi lead me home.

Mama, Phulan, Auntie, and the boys huddle under shawls in the hot, swirling dark. There is no escaping the sand, even indoors, and everything is gritty with the dust that blows with great force through the thatch and around the cracks in the doors and shutters. Mama runs to us and takes the lanterns. She holds me against her for a second.

Her eyes are haunted. I pray Grandfather will die quickly of heart failure and not be skinned alive by the sand and suffocated.

Phulan lifts her hands from over her face, and I can't tell whether she's been crying.

"Your eyes are bright red," she says, looking from Dadi to me and back again.

My vision is blurred, and Phulan leads me to her quilt. Dadi and I both lie down, and Mama dips the corner of her *chadr* into fresh water in which healing desert mint has soaked, and squeezes drops into our eyes. It burns like fire, and I cry out. Even Dadi grunts as Mama gently squeezes the water into the corners of his eyes.

The night is endless. Branches—it feels like entire trees—crash into the walls and thatch. Mama thinks she hears a voice call out. Dadi gets up and lights the lantern. He pushes open the door and goes outside, but there is nothing.

"There is some light out there," he says when he returns a few minutes later. The sand has got into the new watch he bought in Rahimyar Khan. It stopped at five minutes after two. Fear and pain have blurred the time, and we have no way of knowing whether it's morning or afternoon.

The storm goes on for hours more, and we are too exhausted to go outside again until the wind dies. The boys

113

whimper. Sher Dil stays under Mama's skirt and never makes a sound. The rest of us are silent, as if our souls have blown outside with Grandfather, tossed with the dust on the wind.

And then, as suddenly as it began, the storm is over. The wind has torn holes in the thatch, and pale, watery sunlight filters through, even before the wind is quiet. Dadi lifts his head, and dust cascades from the folds of his shawl. His mustache, eyebrows, and eyelashes are coated with pale powder, and the rims and whites of his eyes are blood-red. He looks like a fearful ghost.

Still none of us speaks. Our noses and mouths and throats are parched and caked with dust.

Mama lifts the lid from a pot and pours some water into cups, and I pass them around.

It is late afternoon. I shake the dust from my clothes and hair. Mama wets the end of my *chadr* so I can wipe some of the dust from my eyes, nose, mouth, and ears.

"Quickly," she says, following me to the door. She insists we take a water pot in case we should find Grandfather alive.

The air is calm and cool. The storm has buried all signs of civilization. Even our courtyard looks like a piece of desert, the neat mud walls and storage mounds beaten down and draped with sand.

Outside, the desert has been rearranged. Unfamiliar dunes roll where the land used to lie flat. Stands of shrub and thorn trees are no more. Nothing looks the same. Dadi looks back over his shoulder at the house and fixes a course for the *toba,* where we hope Grandfather will be, somehow safe with the camels.

As we reach the top of each dune, I expect to see water. When we've gone farther than it should be, we split up, Dadi walking into the sun, quivery and pale on the horizon, and I with my back to it. The sand is powdery underfoot, its fresh whiteness an obscenity to me, covering up the devastation it has wrought.

"Grandfather!" I shout, with little hope. "Grandfather, where are you?" If Mithoo is anywhere within hearing, he'll come to the sound of my voice.

According to the legend of the thirsty dead, men lost in the desert tie a turban into the branches of the highest shrubs, then take shelter underneath and wait for help. My eyes scan the few thorn trees, spiky *kharin,* and hardy *pogh* for the pale blue turban Grandfather wore yesterday.

At the foot of a hillock I see a sand-covered lump too small to be a dune, and my heart lurches into my mouth. I turn and shout, "Dadi! Here, Dadi, here!"

I put down the water jar I've been carrying on my head and run toward the thing in the sand.

I fall to my knees and scrape the sand blanket away to find the body of a black baby camel, knees tucked under him, chin on the ground, as if asleep. I pick up his perfect little head and brush the sand from his tightly shut eyes and pinched-down nostrils. Perhaps he'd been sick and unable to move when his mother urged him. He'd just given up here, and the sand had covered him.

"Poor baby," I say softly, stroking the curly dark fur. Where is his mother, and the other camels? And where is the *toba*?

Dadi runs over the hillock. He stops when he sees the dead baby and clucks his tongue. Hands on hips, he looks around with a strange expression on his face.

Suddenly he falls to the ground and begins digging with his hands. The sand flies out behind him in a powdery shower.

"Here!" he says, holding up a handful of damp sand. "This is our *toba*!"

There on the far edge is the thorn tree where I tied Mithoo's goatskin milk bag, where he and I sat after his birth.

I turn back to Dadi, who continues to dig, the sand flying out behind him now in heavy gray clumps.

Finally he sits back on his heels, hands resting on his thighs, breathing heavily. He throws his head back and looks at the sky.

"Allah, Allah," he says softly, tears streaking through the dust on his temples.

I go to his side and squat down to peer into the hole he's dug. A small puddle has formed in the wet sand at the bottom.

"Dadi, there's water enough for a day or two, until we find Grandfather. We'll survive." We'll have to find the camels quickly and bury Grandfather. We have enough three-year-old males to pack and move to the settled area, where Phulan will live the rest of her days after she is wed. Surely the storm will not have filled the wells at Dingarh.

"We'll be all right," I say.

The sun has slipped below the horizon, and there's little color in the sky; the day has stolen quietly away. Dadi stands and I fetch the water pot. Together we walk home, realizing we must leave the desert as soon as possible.

Mama, Auntie, and Phulan have cleaned the houses and shaken the sand from our bedding. They have put the mats back on the floor, and are busy now carrying debris from the courtyard. The little boys are making piles of *khip* to repair the thatch in the morning. Sher Dil watches, his chin on his paws.

Dadi sleeps early, waking for a supper of stew made of leftover meat. The new moon is waxing, and Dadi prepares to go out again in search of Grandfather and the camels, using the stars as guides.

"I'm going with you," I say. Dadi shakes his head.

"You help Mama pack. I'll be back by morning."

Phulan, Mama, and I gather our possessions together again, our cooking pots and plates and cups, our ax and ropes and harnesses, our half-empty water pots, our spindles for making cord, wooden spoons, and whisks.

After several hours Phulan and I drag Grandfather's string cot outside to sleep in the courtyard again, in case he should return during the night.

The moon and stars are brighter than before, the storm having cleared the dust from the air. The shadowless blue-white light is eerie. Mama cries quietly inside. Phulan goes to her, Sher Dil trotting at her heels, and I am asleep before she reaches the door.

Sometime later, in the hours before dawn, the magic symphony of the animals' bells wakes us, *ta-dong-a-room-a-long-chink-a-dong*. I run, apprehensive and groggy with fitful sleep, to the courtyard gate. Dadi's turban glows the same blue-white as the stars in a makeshift harness around the neck of Xhush Dil. The others, fifty or so big camels and dozens of babies, follow in a close knot. They look as if they've just been out grazing. Among them is Mithoo, one of the herd now.

Dadi leads Xhush Dil slowly, gently, for slumped against his hump is Grandfather.

"He's alive!" I shout over my shoulder through the doorway. I can tell by the way his limbs jog. A small moan escapes from Mama's throat, and she is up and running to Grandfather's side. I am close behind, Sher Dil and Phulan tripping over my heels.

Grandfather's fingers are twined tightly in the long, curly hair on Xhush Dil's ample hump. The stocky young camel sinks gently to his knees without command. We pry Grandfather's fingers loose. Phulan and I fetch the string cot, and we carry him on it into the courtyard, where Auntie is building a fire. Mama covers him with a shawl and brings a pot of water.

Grandfather's eyes are open. His cracked lips are parted and he talks soundlessly, rolling his head from side to side. His fingers move restlessly like the claws of a wounded bird. Mama dips the edge of her *chadr* into the water and presses it against his lips. He turns his head away.

I bend my ear closer to his mouth. At first I hear only the faint hiss of softly articulated air.

Grandfather pulls me closer with hands that are powerful for a dying man.

"Kalu," he says. "Make Kalu ready. We must get to Derawar quickly."

I stand and repeat his words. Mama puts her hand on his arm and bends over him.

"Father, we . . ."

"I want to die at Derawar," Grandfather says, his voice stronger now. "The nawab will bury me in a martyr's grave, with turquoise tiles and lapis carvings. He'll plant colored flags at the head of my resting place so people can pray at the grave of a man close to Allah."

Mama looks at Dadi.

"We'll leave by first light, Father," says Dadi. "Phulan, help your mother. Shabanu, come with me to get water."

Grandfather closes his eyes. His hands stop moving and lie limp on the shawl that covers him. Mama kneels by his side for a moment, stroking his head and watching him closely.

"Dalil Abassi," says Mama, addressing Dadi formally for the first time that I can remember. Dadi turns wearily toward her.

"I found him huddled among the camels at Mujara-wala *Toba*, where the dunes are high," Dadi says. "It's a miracle he survived."

"He'll be lucky to live through the night," Mama says.

"We'll take him to Derawar," Dadi says. "We can't stay here without water. Let him die in peace."

"The camels?"

"We've lost only two or three, and they may turn up."

Mama nods and turns back to take up her vigil over Grandfather while Phulan and Auntie bustle through the houses and courtyard, stacking quilts and pots, wrapping utensils in bundles, and hauling out the camel saddles.

The Thirsty Dead

Dadi and I squeeze enough water from the sand to fill one goatskin. Our half-full water pots are round and fat, sweating and red, tempting our thirsty eyes.

The light glints orange on Mama's nose disk as she ties the pots with goathair twine very carefully, as if they hold gems. She hands them up to Dadi, who stands in front of the hump of a gentle old female camel. He handles the pots gingerly, tying them securely to the wooden frame of the saddle and packing clothing and quilts around them so they won't shatter.

We load Xhush Dil last with the most important cargo: Phulan's dowry chest and Grandfather.

Grandfather lies on his string cot, eyes wide and sightless; his once-strong hands, now curled and covered with waxy skin, search restlessly over the pale green quilt that lies across his chest. On his head is the khaki fez of the nawab's army, its tassel crumpled, the felt faded and torn.

In its center is the bronze star for bravery, brass rays surrounding it like a holy emblem. He earned it for leading the charge at Kutch.

Grandfather's lips move wordlessly, and Mama and I stop our rushed packing every few minutes to soothe him.

When it is time to leave, Dadi and Mama carry Grandfather on his cot beyond the courtyard, and I follow, leading Xhush Dil. It is our custom never to get onto the camels in front of our house for fear we'll never return. In normal times it is sad to leave home. Now it is unbearable.

"Uuusshhhshh," I say softly, and the young camel sinks to his knees with barely a whisper in the sand. Dadi loops cords around the head and foot of the cot, and we hoist Grandfather to where his weight balances the dowry chest on the other side of the wooden pack frame.

Xhush Dil gets to his feet again in a movement so fluid I think he must know the value of his cargo. Dadi lifts the glass of the lantern and blows out the flame. The eerie blue of near dawn enfolds us, and we move off without looking back.

We pass the place where our raised mud prayer platform stood until yesterday, its delicately molded *mehrab* facing toward Mecca. Dadi looks at the mound of sand that covers it as if he thinks he should stop to pray, but we keep walking.

Mithoo's head is several inches higher than my own. The bell on the new cord around his neck clangs solemnly as he trots beside me, his feet making no sound in the wind-fluffed sand. The other camels move in syncopation, their loads swaying side to side and back and forth.

As the sun rises, the breeze picks up, printing shivery lines on the sand. We walk, talking little, until heat suffuses the air. We stop once, and Mama ties a *chadr* to the cords holding Grandfather's cot and lets it drape over him to keep out the blinding white sun.

When we stop in the shade of a thorn tree, the camels stretch their necks to browse. Dadi climbs the tree to cut fodder for Xhush Dil so he won't disturb Grandfather, whose hands are quiet again under the *chadr*.

I climb up on the camel's hump to fill a battered metal cup from the water pot. I hand it carefully down to Phulan. Her face is pale, eyes dark, her lips drawn. She hands the cup up to Mama, who sits astride Xhush Dil's hump and leans over to offer Grandfather a drink. I peer into the pot. The water has receded another inch.

Grandfather won't drink, but each of the rest of us takes

a swallow. We pass the cup until it's empty. The two sips I get taste silvery, cutting the parchment bitterness in my throat and leaving me desperate for more.

After we have rested, Phulan and I walk out ahead of the others looking for *sito,* a fragrant grass with roots that run deep in the sand and are sweet with water.

"Do you remember when Uncle led us to Dingarh?" Phulan asks. I do remember. We'd been three days with no water, and Uncle found *sito* far from the track in the area of the largest dunes. Phulan and I head off toward the rolling sand, where the dunes cast peaked and fluted shadows like waves frozen on a sea.

We climb the side of one dune, our bare feet sliding in the scalding sand. Beneath us the desert's silvery shrubs cast a haze over the desert. But no *sito.*

Phulan makes a sound that catches in her throat and grasps my arm. Over our heads on the tallest of dunes stands a *kharin* bush, its branches blown bare of the lovely pink dog-faced flowers that bloomed before the storm. From its top green-stick branches, a pale blue banner flutters on the rising heat.

Phulan is terrified of ghosts. A traveler has tied his turban to the highest branch and should be waiting in the shade for someone to find him and bring water. But nobody is under the bush.

The turban is faded, its ends tattered. It probably has been there since before the storm. A shudder of horror skips across my shoulders. I start forward, but Phulan pulls me back.

"What if he's dead?" Her eyes are wide, her fingers flutter.

The legend of the thirsty dead says if you find a thirsty man too late to save his life, he'll moan and clamor, his ghost following you the rest of your life.

"Get Dadi," I tell her, and turn back toward the tree.

"Shabanu!" She is terrified.

"Go!" I shout at her. "Don't be such a baby."

She looks at the turban and back at me.

"Go!"

She turns and runs down the other side of the dune, her *chadr* a red flame behind her as her feet slip down the hot sand, raising powdery gray clouds.

I look back at the *kharin*, its branches prickly with tiny thorns. The breeze swirls pillows of dust around the dune and hisses through the branches. It's a desolate place to die. The turban catches, convulses in the wind, and is free again. On the other side of the shimmering white dune, a brown leather sandal lies flat on the sand, as if someone has taken it off in a hurry. Beside it, flapping lazily, is the corner of the dead man's *lungi,* the only part of him that has escaped the sandy grave.

I have no inclination to disturb him. I sit under the sheltering curve of the dune, wondering how death will come to Grandfather, to Dadi—to all of us.

Dadi hurries around the dune, a jug of water under his arm. I help him push the sand aside. Not very deep a young man lies curled on his side, his face calm as if he'd fallen asleep in the storm. Dadi brushes the sand from his thick hair and the brows over his deep-set eyes. His face is strong and gentle, and an odd twist of grief turns in my heart. He was someone's brother—by the grace of God he might have been my own.

I climb into the prickly shrub to retrieve his turban. Dadi turns the man's face toward Mecca and chants the prayers a family says for its dead. He pours water into his palm and sprinkles it over the lifeless face as a token of the ritual washing of the dead. He wraps the turban like a shroud about the man's head and shoulders, and we sit silently for a moment, wishing his soul well on its way.

We heap more sand over him. As we turn to leave, Dadi reaches into the jar and sprinkles a handful of water over the head of the grave in the hope that it will quench the man's thirsty spirit.

The jackals will be hungry after the storm, and it won't be long before they find him. I shiver again and wish we could make him a better grave.

Dadi rests his hand on my shoulder as we walk silently to the thorn trees where the camels and our family wait in the shade.

We eat *chapati*s, talking little, and wait for the hottest part of the day to pass. Even the boys and Sher Dil are sprawled in the shade of a kneeling camel, fast asleep. Thank God the usual pestilence of flies has been driven away by the storm, and I can nap without covering my face.

Dadi sits beside Grandfather, talking to him quietly. Perhaps he is telling him the thousand things I'd like to tell Dadi that I love about him—and know would embarrass him. Grandfather's fingers begin to move over his chest again with the nimbleness of near death.

Mama is calm as she talks about Grandfather.

"He was a strong and brave man. I was terrified of him when he asked my father if I would marry Dadi. But he was gentle as well, and he always made me feel like his own daughter."

I feel oddly detached as I listen to Mama's soothing voice, her slender hand stroking my head in her lap. Mithoo stands over us, and the muted melody of the camel bells lulls me to sleep.

The sun is hazed with sand picked up by the afternoon wind skidding over the dunes. When it falls lower in the sky, the air cools slightly. We prepare to walk again, and I go to Grandfather's side.

"We'll be at Derawar before dark," I tell him. "Don't worry. The nawab will receive you."

I look at Mama, defying her to say it won't be so. Even I doubt the nawab will remember an old soldier.

We reach the old fort just as the sun slips behind the dunes, and the last pink fingers of light burnish its forty graceful turrets.

The nawab's green and red flag flutters beside the green banner of Pakistan, and we stand on the hill looking over the lake built by the nawab of a hundred years ago for his ladies to paddle little boats across. The wind has died, and the last daylight leaves a silvery skin on the water. Mama lifts Grandfather's head to see the marble dome and vaulted minarets of the nawab's mosque beyond the fort's massive brick walls.

"We won't disturb Nawab-*sahib* until morning," Grandfather says, then falls back on his pillow, his hands and face relaxed for the first time since we left.

The camels move on, their only sound the *kachinnik, kachinnik* of their bracelets, the gentle thong of their bells, and the creaking of goathair cords against their wooden saddles. We stop beside a collection of torn lean-tos built by other nomads. Our reed mats will make walls and a small courtyard. The camp is within walking distance of the well. Phulan and I have been collecting firewood over the last several miles, and Auntie makes a fire while Mama unrolls the mats.

Xhush Dil sinks quietly to his knees. Dadi and I lower the dowry trunk and the cot on which Grandfather sleeps. We have enough water in the goatskin until tomorrow. At first light Dadi, Xhush Dil, and I will go to the well. Only then will we know whether the water is sweet. The well out here on the edge of the settlement is least likely to have good water. But our goatskins will be empty, and we are so thirsty we will drink even salty water. God willing, the monsoon will not fail this year.

My stomach tightens and my throat burns thinking of the month ahead until the monsoon rains come—thinking that we'll drink salt water and the grass will shrivel and the camel's milk will dry up and the babies will grow weak.

It will be a good omen if the drought ends in time for Phulan's wedding. I say a silent prayer that the rains will come and that Hamir will be kind to her.

Derawar

"Grandfather is dead, Shabanu," Mama says, leaning over me, shaking me awake in the dark. Dadi leaps up from his quilt and turns Grandfather's head toward Mecca so his soul can pray.

Everyone is calm, and in the morning it seems we all had known Grandfather's soul would take flight once it reached Derawar.

Dadi washes Grandfather's thin and wasted body with the last of our water, chanting prayers for the dead. There's no time to spare. It's shortly after dawn, and the heat of the day will be fierce. As he and Mama wrap the shroud around the body, Dadi chants softly in his wood-smoke voice.

Grandfather's worn foot with the split toenail lies inert and topples sideways like a sack of lentils as Dadi lifts the body to slip the white seamless cloth under him. I bandaged that toe for Grandfather. This lifeless foot will never again feel such a thing as a split toenail, and I grieve for it, as if it embodies all of Grandfather.

Auntie, Mama, and Phulan stay to fetch water at the well and to pray. Grandfather is laid out on his string cot, such a small and insignificant little form for the tall and strong warrior of his stories.

The devil sun creeps into the doorway, chasing the chill from the dark reed enclosure. We must hurry, Dadi and I, to find a burial place before the heat . . . how we would hate to think of his body stinking, swelling up. Oh, we must hurry!

We ride Xhush Dil and the gentle old female camel to the graveyard on the other side of the fort, at the end of the village where the bodies of the nawab's family and the heroes of the army lie. Over a broken stone wall patched in places with barbed wire, we see the martyrs' graves—white marble inlaid with turquoise and lapis and tiles, some inscribed with gold—glistening in the sun. Flags flutter over the heads of the long, mounded tombs to mark the place where the troubled and needy might find a place to pray beside a spirit that has influence with God.

The blue tiled domes of the elaborate tombs of the nawabs' wives cast bulbous shadows across the empty graveyard. A crow balances on a *kharin* bush that has crept up between the gravestones in the yard, his mouth open but silent, eyes blinking.

A broken gate of wood tips on its hinges. A big brass lock holds together a rusting iron chain. Nobody is in the graveyard, and we turn toward the village.

As I turn the camel into the sun, an old man with a crooked foot hobbles toward us, leaning on a stick, his features indistinct against the bright haze forming over the desert. He is a hand's length shorter than I am.

"*Asalaam-o-Aleikum,*" says Dadi. "Where is the keeper of the tombs?"

The man touches his fingertips to his turban in silent greeting.

"I am Sulaiman, keeper of the tombs," the old man replies in a voice worn raw by the desert.

Dadi steps onto the strong *U* of Xhush Dil's neck and jumps to the ground. Each of them touches the other's fingertips lightly in a stranger's greeting.

"My father is Jindwadda Ali Abassi of the old nawab's camel corps," says Dadi. "He has died in the night. It is his wish to be buried among his brothers who fell in battle in the service of the nawab."

The old man tips his head as if he hasn't understood.

132

Dadi waits. A fly buzzes lazily over the little man's turban, the first I've seen since the storm.

"Nobody has been buried here in twenty years," he says finally. "Except His Highness's wife, whose tomb is grandest of all."

"Is there a place for an old and faithful soldier who wears the medal of bravery on his fez?" asks Dadi.

Again the twisted little man doesn't speak, and the sun, still hovering over the horizon, scorches my shoulders. I think of the heat corrupting Grandfather's body. We must hurry, we must hurry, we must hurry!

"The estate of the nawab is being contested," he says. "Nobody has been allowed on the property for five years, since the dispute went to court."

"Who is in charge?" asks Dadi.

"Permission to enter can be given by the commissioner in Bahawalpur," he says, scratching his yellow beard. "But only VIPs are allowed in to see the fort and tombs."

"Is there nobody here who can make a decision?" Dadi speaks patiently, but I can tell he is growing angry with the stubborn old man who wants to show his meager power.

"The keeper of the fort," says the gnome, fumbling in his dirty tunic for a cigarette. "He can contact the nawab's son, who lives in Lahore; he's a member of the Provincial Assembly, and . . ."

Dadi turns Xhush Dil toward the fort and I follow, and the old man hobbles a few steps after us.

"There's no room here, anyway!" he shouts after us. "The nawab doesn't even have an army now, except for the bodyguard that protects his family from his enemies . . ." His voice is lost as we leave him behind with his importance.

"Your grandfather is too good a man to lie in such company. He would have given his life for them, yet they deny him a decent grave," Dadi says, his voice rough with bitterness.

"We must try, Dadi. Grandfather wanted it. We owe him a try, at least."

Dadi doesn't speak, but we head back around the tombs, behind the village, a scrappy place of mud huts with crude drawings of animals and men, stars and moons whitewashed on the walls, bare-bottomed children playing among the thorns, dogs running out to yap at the camels' heels.

We pass the mosque where Dadi and I had gone to pray on our way to Sibi. The white marble domes glisten like fat, juicy onions.

The camels walk slowly up the long, cobbled ramp that leads to the huge wooden doors, just as Grandfather had described them, the tips of sword blades at the top to keep out the elephants of the Raja of Bikaner.

A door of inch-thick bars stands between us and the wooden gates. Dadi calls out, and a thin old man, brown as mud, with a white beard, stoops through the three-foot doorway of the guardroom behind the bars. He slips a fez like Grandfather's—but red—over his shaved brown head.

"Yes, sir, can I help you?" he asks, squinting up at Dadi through the bars. Dadi jumps down and they exchange greetings. Through the ancient guard's pure white mustache, three long teeth protrude. Grandfather has told me about those who wear the red fez. They are the nawab's personal guard. Has the gnome told us the truth about the nawab's bodyguards in Lahore? Perhaps this is the only one left: he is as old as Grandfather.

He is Shahzada (his name is a mother's wish that her son had been born a king), and he confirms what the gnome Sulaiman has told us. The estate and the son of the nawab, as well as several of his cousins, all claim not only the fort at Derawar but the nawab's palace in Bahawalpur and the graveyard and all of the nawab's lands that remained after Pakistan and India were separated.

"Cholistan was once home to a great civilization," he tells us. "Now it is just a patch of sand with weeds. But the nawab envisioned pumping the great Hakra River up from under the desert and making this into a fertile valley once again."

Dadi and I are interested, but we explain that we must hurry to find a burial place for Grandfather. He seems truly sorry not to be able to help. He directs us to the village of the tomb maker. We thank Shahzada and ask him to our camp to share our dinner. It's our custom to feed villagers when there is a death. But the village is unfriendly, and Shahzada is the only helpful soul we've found here.

The rest of the day drags in a blur of heat and frantic

but frustrated effort. First we go to the maker of tombs, but his daughter tells us he has gone to another village. Is there no one else who makes tombs? No, she says, only her father.

So Dadi and I go to the dried up *toba* and dig through the sand down to the clay. The old bed of the Hakra River is hard as rock, with shells still embedded in it, preserved by the desert air. We break up chunks of the clay and pound it into powder, then carry it in wheat sacks to the camels to be hauled back to camp.

Mama and Auntie have collected fresh cow dung, and fortunately there is water in the well. Our goatskins and jars are full.

We load Grandfather, rigid now under his shroud, still on the string cot, onto Xhush Dil with the mud and the cow dung and the water, and set out into the desert to find a burial spot where the jackals, foxes, and wolves won't find his body.

In the heat of the afternoon, we dig six feet into the ground, Dadi and I taking turns. Mama and Phulan mix the powdered clay, cow dung, water, and sand into desert cement, and we pave the hole as we work to keep it from filling up again.

Within sight of his beloved Derawar, we lay Grandfather gently under a bush in a solitary grave. Dadi turns him on his right side so that he faces Mecca, and each of us throws a handful of Cholistan sand over him, whispering a prayer and saying good-bye.

Phulan and Auntie cut up remnants left from the wedding dresses to make flags to plant on long sticks at the head of Grandfather's grave. As the sun sets we bury him, chanting prayers, helping his soul on its path to heaven, and shaping the cement into a fine burial mound. Finally we secure the sticks with the colored flags at his head, where pilgrims might pray.

We walk forty paces from the grave, where we say the last prayers, for already the angels are questioning Grandfather.

When it's over, we are relieved that his suffering has ended and that his body is safe in the ground. But my heart still carries the promise we made to bury him beside those with whom he fought.

Conversation turns to what we should do next.

"It's too soon to go to Mehrabpur," says Mama, taking charge of our plans. "Hamir and his family don't expect us until Ramadan."

It is two weeks before the fasting month of Ramadan, still a month before the monsoon rains refill the *tobas*.

"I'll not stay here!" Dadi says. "I'm happy Grandfather's grave does not lie in the village."

Mama nods.

"But there is little choice," she says, and that is that. We will stay here until we move to Mehrabpur just before Ramadan to prepare for the wedding.

The water at the Derawar well is salty. The camels drink little, and my throat is beginning to ache again with thirst.

When we are back in camp, we resume the normal rhythm of our lives and it soothes us. The boys play with

Sher Dil. Mama becomes cross with them and sends them outside. We make tea, and with milk and sugar the salt water is not so difficult to drink.

Mama and Phulan talk about final preparations for the wedding. I listen to their chatter about dresses and bangles and furniture and plates while I mix the gray salty water into flour for our evening *chapatis*. They never once mention Hamir or how Phulan should behave toward Hamir's mother when the wedding is over and they all are living together—everything *I* want to know about marriage.

An odd but pleasant tightening in my belly makes my hands skip a beat in kneading the dough as I think of Murad's serious, dark eyes, and I wonder what it will be like to see him again, knowing in a year he and I will marry.

Outside the circle of our campfire we hear someone approach, singing. Dadi stands and greets Shahzada with a warm embrace. The old guard is wearing a faded tunic over a *lungi,* and there is no sign of his red fez. His bald head is glossy with the orange glow of the campfire.

"Where have you buried Abassi-*bhai*?" Dadi is pleased Shahzada uses the affectionate term meaning "brother" for his old colleague.

Dadi tells him, and the old man nods.

"I will watch over the grave," he says.

Dadi and Shahzada talk about the drought. We keep few sheep and no cows or goats. But Shahzada says people are beginning to leave the desert with their animals because the grasses have withered and there is little left for them to eat. Camels can eat almost anything, and our animals haven't had trouble with sickness and hunger yet.

"The old nawab," Shahzada says, "believed we could pump water from under the ground onto the land. He used to say, 'You see how flowers bloom in the sand when there is water? This is not desert. This is land without water.' "

A shepherd plays a sweet melody on his flute far out in the desert, calling his flock to graze. They respond with the muted ringing of their bells, ghostly as they pass among the dunes.

Grandfather's body lies out under the stars, alone for the first time since the sandstorm. I wonder whether his soul is near enough to hear the flute or, now that it is free, whether he can see inside my heart and know I am thinking of him.

"Shahzada-*sahib*," I say, "could you help us keep a promise to my grandfather?"

"Shabanu," Dadi says, a warning in his voice.

"I know it was impossible to bury him in the nawab's graveyard," I rush on. "Would you put his fez and sword somewhere in an honored place?"

"Oh, could you?" asks Mama.

Shahzada tells us of a tomb built for a general who died in battle and whose body was never found.

"There are other relics in the empty tomb," he says. "It

is a beautiful one with blue and white tiles, lapis with gold script. That would be an appropriate place for the fez and sword of a man who won the medal for bravery."

Grandfather's relics will rest with those of his brothers, and finally his soul will rest in peace.

Ramadan

As the days pass the well water dwindles, and the people of Derawar pray for early rain. We decide to leave for the edge of the desert and fresh sweet water. We will reach Mehrabpur, where we will plan Phulan's wedding, before Ramadan. This will be my first year to keep the sacred fast, as children aren't required to do so until they stop growing.

I wonder how I can survive the heat when I can't eat

or drink. Not even a sip of this wretched, gray, salty water! I ask Mama.

"It's a matter of faith and will," she says. I am not satisfied, but I say nothing and return to my work.

The morning of our departure we bring the camels to the well when it's our turn to draw water. They stand in a ring, necks extended, waiting for us to fill the trough.

I uncoil the rope on the stanchion over the well and hook it to Xhush Dil's wooden saddle. Phulan lays the rope across the pulley and drops the goatskin down, down into the darkness of the well until we hear it splash. She tests the rope to see if the goatskin is full, then sucks in her breath when the rope bites into the soft flesh of her palms.

"You take Xhush Dil," I say, taking the rope from her. How will she manage as the wife of a poor farmer—one who will need her help in the fields? She looks back at me as I test the rope. It digs into my palms, but the pain is useful and therefore good.

I signal her to move Xhush Dil forward, but she stands still, looking uncertain. So I tell the camel to pull. I feel an urge to shake her, to put sense into her lazy, romantic head. Xhush Dil strains forward, and the water-filled bucket rises up inside the well, dripping salt water along the mud walls as it comes.

Phulan lets out a dainty yelp. I raise my eyes from the ascending goatskin in time to see Xhush Dil snatch her *chadr* from her head and wave it like a banner, his front legs stepping out before him, his neck straining against the weight of the filled bucket. For the first time in weeks, laughter bubbles up into my throat, and I barely manage to holler to him to stop before he pulls the whole stanchion away from the well. I laugh until my belly aches.

Even Auntie smiles. Xhush Dil stands in place, tossing the *chadr* like a flag, as though he were a carnival clown. I whoop until tears stream from my eyes, and I clutch my stomach. Phulan, too, shrieks with laughter, and it feels so good, as if life will go on after all.

The wind whips our skirts around us and plasters our tunics to our chests as we walk from the camp. The voyage seems like a haze of sand, the sun a pallid disk over the dunes. We pass dozens of animals felled by hunger and thirst on the track to Mehrabpur. The bodies of six camels lie, ropes still joining them nose to tail, their feet raised as if they walk in death. They are partially covered by blowing sand; the meat has dried on their bones, robbing the foxes and jackals of a meal.

At the end of the second day a breeze bears the overripe smell of green across the desert. A line of vegetation marks the irrigation channel built by Hamir's father on his twenty-five acres. Turning the desert to farmland killed him, crippling him with old age before the years had a chance. An image of Phulan, her black-draped figure stooped over the field ahead, stands before the eye of my imagination.

Dadi breaks away and rides to the oasis to greet Hamir and Murad. In the distance a group of figures seems to float toward us across the desert on a shimmering lake of reflected heat. Three of them wear white, the color of mourning.

Bibi Lal, Hamir's mother, is a large woman with wise eyes and pendulous breasts. She carries a sweating pot of water. Bibi Lal's husband has been dead for two monsoons now, but she will wear white to mourn him the rest of her life.

Her daughter-in-law Kulsum walks behind Bibi Lal, an infant clutched against her shoulder. Kulsum's small daughter walks beside her, a bare-bottomed two-year-old boy on her hip; her five-year-old son runs beside them, driving two goats with a stick. Kulsum is a few years older than Phulan. She is thin and pale, with deep lines around her mouth and eyes.

Kulsum wears white to mourn her husband, Lal Khan, the elder brother of Hamir and Murad. His body was found last year in a well that belongs to the landowner Nazir Mohammad.

Bibi Lal raises her large, work-worn hand to her forehead and welcomes us.

"How I wish my husband, peace be with him, were here!" she says. "He would be so happy to see the daughters of his beloved cousin marry our sons."

"My husband thought of him as a brother," Mama says. "He loves your sons as if they were his own."

Bibi Lal folds Phulan into her arms and kisses her. Mama looks relieved. Many young women come to their husband's houses as slaves to their mothers-in-law.

"Sakina!" Bibi Lal shouts to her young daughter. "Stop dawdling and bring the ladle!"

The water is sweet and cool. Never have I tasted such silvery freshness! There is plenty; Bibi Lal pours cup after cup for us until we can drink no more.

Everyone focuses attention on Phulan. But I watch Kulsum and wonder whether bearing children will rob my sister of her beauty while she is still a girl.

The women show us where to make our camp within walking distance of the canal.

"Come here," says Bibi Lal, "under the trees."

"We prefer to be in the open," says Mama. "We are desert people!" Mama's teeth dazzle white in her dark face, and Bibi Lal gives in.

Bibi Lal insists on helping us make camp. She sends Sakina to fetch extra baskets and water for mixing mud and rolls her sleeves above her elbows. We build frames of cut tree branches and tie reed mats against them. We thatch the roofs with *khip,* build a mud platform to serve as kitchen and a second platform for prayers, with a small carved slab at one end that faces toward Mecca. We sing and laugh as we work.

The clouds remain for several days after our fasting begins. We neither eat nor drink until the sun goes down, when we break our fast with tea. The first two days I feel dizzy and sleepy, but soon I am accustomed to an empty stomach. After prayers we have a meal of lentils, yogurt, and *chapatis.*

Dadi sees Hamir and Murad every day. He brings news of them to the campfire. Hamir has built a cottage for Phulan on their land. A cottage! With an indoor kitchen, a separate room for sleeping, and a courtyard surrounded by a strong wall. The women are covering it now with mud, straw, and cow dung.

Phulan's eyes dance with excitement.

"Have you seen him?" she asks Dadi. A girl never refers to the man she will marry by name.

Dadi smiles and strokes her hair.

"Hamir is noble and strong and handsome," he replies, and Phulan claps her hands, then folds them over her smile, half in pleasure, half in embarrassment.

We won't see Hamir and Murad until the wedding day, and even then I'm not certain I will see Murad. I wonder what he looks like now. Has he grown handsome, or do his ears still stick out? Is his neck muscular now like Hamir's?

I strain my eyes toward the fields looking for Murad when I take the camels to graze. Then Dadi tells me I mustn't take the camels out alone.

"You must stay with Phulan every second," he tells me.

"But she won't come with me to graze the camels!" Daydreaming has overtaken Phulan's every waking minute.

"You mustn't go alone."

"Why not?" I demand. I am filled with dread that I might be kept from the camels and from wandering where I please.

146

"Do as I say!" He turns and walks away.

"Dadi, I have so little time." My voice is barely a whisper. I'm not sure he heard. But he turns slowly toward me.

"Nazir Mohammad has returned from the city," he says.

"Why should we fear him?" Dadi squints at me for a moment, then squats in the sand and gestures for me to join him.

"This land was a patch of dust, good only for browsing camels, when Hamir's father bought it," he says. "Nazir Mohammad didn't care about it then. When they dug the canal and planted crops, Nazir watched to see how the corn grew. The harder they worked, the more the land produced. And the angrier Nazir grew. Then one day Lal Khan didn't come home. Hamir and Murad searched every inch of the land.

"A month passed and Kulsum gave birth to her fourth child. Still no trace of Lal Khan. One day her son came running into the courtyard shouting that there was a terrible smell in Nazir's old well. Kulsum dropped the baby into her daughter's arms and ran with Hamir and Murad to the well. They found the remains of Lal Khan, his slippers pointing toward the sky."

"What does Nazir want?" My voice sounds thick and strange.

"Nazir demands a quarter of their crops as compensation for farming the land. Hamir and Murad have stamped deeds, but the court has taken three years to rule. Perhaps

147

Nazir is influencing the judge. He takes every opportunity to cause trouble."

"Shouldn't we tell Phulan?" I ask.

"Why ruin her wedding?" His eyes look weary. "She'll have the rest of her life to worry. No, just stay with her and be sure to let your mother and me know where you are."

We spend the next week cooking sweets for the wedding, making dresses for the women of Hamir's family, and dyeing turbans in bright colors for the men. I drag Phulan out to the fields with me to cut grass for fodder with long, curved sickles. I tell her we have little time to be together, and she comes willingly. I watch over my shoulder as I work.

Kulsum and Sakina bring the children to visit us as we rest in the afternoons. Bibi Lal is kind to Kulsum, and people say she is lucky. But she will be a widow forever, and her grief shows always, even when she smiles.

When the cottage for Hamir and Phulan is finished, Bibi Lal, Kulsum, and Sakina invite us to inspect it and have tea. We bring gifts: sweets made with nuts and raisins, scarves that we've embroidered with colored silk and mirrors, and dried mushrooms.

Phulan's eyes grow wide when she sees the house, a square brown box with mud walls and a thatched roof. It's like any farmhouse at the edge of the desert, but this one is Phulan's. She turns to us and her eyes are damp, her lips parted. She is speechless.

Bibi Lal clucks at her and urges us inside. She takes the baby from Kulsum and settles him in a sling tied to the cottage rafters. She sends the older children outside to play and brings out a beautiful bottle with a silver base and stopper. She opens the top and passes it around for us to smell the sweet fragrance inside.

"It's jasmine oil. You must rub Phulan with it in the days before the wedding," Bibi Lal tells Mama. "Add some cumin, and her skin will be fragrant and smooth and golden." Phulan blushes with pleasure.

After tea Bibi Lal calls us outside, where tins of white paint sit open and glaring in the morning sun. On a cloth beside the tins are sticks with short goathairs tied to one end. Bibi Lal hands Kulsum a brush and asks her to begin the ceremony of decorating the house where Hamir and Phulan will conceive their sons.

Kulsum paints a fish for fertility, her hand deft and sure. She dots the fish's eye and hands the brush to Sakina, who paints circles intertwined for harmony in the family, her tongue sticking out the side of her mouth as she concentrates. I paint camels for wealth and hand the brush to Mama. She paints a row of lines with arms and legs and appendages that indicate the sons she wishes for Phulan.

As we paint we talk about the cousins who will come to the wedding. Soon we have paint on our faces and in our hair. We laugh and chatter like sisters.

Phulan is not supposed to paint her own house, for fear

it will bring bad luck. When we finish we sit back to admire our work.

The image of Kulsum, tired and anemic, haunts me. And as we leave, a twinge of regret that I have not seen Murad pinches my heart.

The Landlord

Sharma and Fatima are due to arrive within a week, and
Phulan and I talk happily about seeing them as we fill our
water pots at the canal.

"Sharma says I'll have a son the first year," says Phulan. I hand a water jar up to her, but she's looking at the
tops of the trees.

"Phulan!" She takes the jar from my hand and gives
me an empty one.

151

"She says if I eat plenty of lentils and milk and butter he'll be fat and healthy. I hope he looks like his father."

Hamir is as different from Murad as I am from Phulan. He is wild, like Dadi says I am. He loves horses and rides them hard. But he's insensitive, coming back with his horse lathered and breathing heavily. He is handsome and tall like Phulan, and impatient, a dreamer. I've always liked him less than Murad. He is the older brother by three years. He never had time to join our children's games. But he is decent. I remember Murad going to him to decide when two of us claimed to have won a race. He offered us the choice of splitting the prize, a melon, or running the race again.

Sharma's words play through my mind, and the truth steals like a stranger into my heart: Phulan and I are very lucky for desert girls, marrying not only decent men but men who have land, who are richer than anyone in our family.

"Don't you think he is handsome?" asks Phulan.

I consider for a moment. He was seventeen when we saw him last year at Adil's wedding. He had a thick mustache and broad, strong hands. He stood very straight. But handsome? As compared with Murad's thin neck and protruding ears, I'd have to say yes.

"I suppose so," I reply. How strange that we barely remember how they look, when very soon Phulan will see Hamir every day for the rest of her life.

I hand Phulan another pot. When the pots are full, Phulan loads two pots on my head and I leave her behind to wash the cloths she uses during her monthly bleeding. She makes a major production of it, to show how grown-up she is, and I turn my back on her as she hums over her washing beside the canal.

Xhush Dil, Mithoo, and I walk slowly down the canal path toward our camp as the clouds part for a moment just before the sun sets, leaving a sheen like sun-ripened melon on the water.

The air cools rapidly and mist rises from the canal, making ghostly shadows of the grasses and bushes against the opal sky. Perhaps this will be a good place to live after all.

"Who is this?" asks a smooth, deep voice from the bottom of the canal bank. I look down at a fat man in a silk tunic and drawstring trousers. He leans on a hand-carved shotgun. Laughter booms out from the bushes.

My heart quickens with the realization I've disobeyed and left Phulan alone. I lean back against Xhush Dil's shoulder as if he'll protect me. Another man with hard eyes, younger and slimmer than the first, steps out from behind a tree. He also has a gun. Both men wear elaborately embroidered caps, finely woven vests, and gold watches. A third man appears, and a fourth—a young man, still part boy.

"How about this one?" the fat man asks the boy-man.

"She's just a child, Uncle," he replies, looking me over, up and down with eyes that have seen a great deal for one his age.

I cover my face, for the men look as if they are taking

me apart with their eyes. For the first time I'm grateful that I am small and not so elegant as Phulan. But she will come this same way in a moment, and they will want to take her with them, surely as the mustard blooms in spring!

"That one!" says the slim man, pointing a manicured finger up the canal.

Phulan walks slowly along the bank, her bangles clinking on her brown arm, slender hips swaying, the basket of knotted, wet cloths atop the water jar on her head, another round jar under her arm. She hasn't seen the men yet, and she looks beautiful and dreamy with the lowering sun glowing behind her like a halo.

The men watch as Phulan catches up with me, her face uncovered and lovely, her nose disk glinting in reflected sunlight, her graceful, pale fingers molded around the curves of the water jars. When she sees the men she stops, but she doesn't seem alarmed.

"Yes," says the fat one. "The one who bags the most quails gets that one." There is more laughter.

"What about me?" asks one of them. "I shot the only blue bull. I should have her."

"Well?" asks the fat one, turning to Phulan. "We'll pay you handsomely—land, jewelry, money, anything you like."

Phulan puts her hand on her hip and thrusts it forward, a defiant look on her face. Her breasts are high and firm under her thin cotton tunic.

Oh, I could kill her. What is she thinking? Mama has warned us dozens of times: Nazir Mohammad, the landowner, has hunting parties. He offers each of his guests a girl, usually a tenant from his land, for the time they are with him. When the man is finished with her, he gives her cash and sends her back to her family. Some people are grateful for the money and are willing to forget the indignity. But Hamir and Dadi won't, I'm certain.

"We're not tenants," I say to him, poking Phulan sharply with my elbow as I step in front of her. "You have no claim over us!"

Nazir Mohammad laughs, and a diamond ring sparkles on his finger.

"This little one is a hot-blooded thing," he says, coming closer.

We are trapped. Both of us have jars of water on our heads. We can't turn and run away from this leering fat man. The thought of him sweating over Phulan makes me ill. I snap my head forward, tossing the water jugs down the side of the embankment, and the men scatter as the jars break, splashing mud onto the landlord's silken trousers.

He curses and the others laugh. I push the jar from Phulan's head down the embankment, and Nazir Mohammad curses and stumbles in an effort to scramble up the embankment after us, his fat bottom wobbling behind him. The others laugh at his clumsiness, and his face is blue with rage.

Phulan drops the other clay water jar. She is immobilized with fear. Without having Xhush Dil kneel I swing up onto his neck and pull Phulan up behind me. She is not so agile as I am, and her legs dangle as she tries to pull herself up. I stand and work my way up onto Xhush Dil's hump, pulling Phulan high enough to grab his neck. Our skirts hike up with our struggle, and Nazir splutters, his feet and trousers muddy, near the top of the embankment. The other men bend at the waist and slap their thighs with thick, hairy hands, tears of helpless mirth streaming down their cheeks.

Mithoo is alarmed now and dances around Xhush Dil as if the big camel were his mother. I urge Xhush Dil into a trot along the canal path, deciding these men must not see where we are going. But they are laughing so hard they aren't watching. They crumple against one another, holding their stomachs as Xhush Dil gathers speed. We gallop along, Mithoo struggling to keep up but falling farther behind with each of Xhush Dil's long strides.

Nazir Mohammad has made it to the top of the embankment, cursing in rage and shaking his gun in the air.

Terrified that we are leaving him behind, Mithoo bolts from the canal path and heads straight for our camp. Our makeshift shelters look like desert shrubbery, except that Mama has started a fire, and a dot of orange glints beside the clumps of matting, a thin curl of bluish smoke rising against the early evening sky.

I look back over my shoulder, and the landlord and his friends stand atop the embankment, watching Mithoo's wild-legged progress toward our camp.

Still I urge Xhush Dil along the canal path, hoping they won't see where we are going, but my heart knows that they will follow at their leisure to take Phulan away.

When we are out of their sight, I turn Xhush Dil down the embankment. Phulan holds on to me with all her might, terrified at the speed of our flight.

Dadi meets us, his camel walking from the other direction, fodder slung in sacks on either side of the animal's hump. I jump to the ground beside our lean-to before Xhush Dil kneels, and Phulan falls to the dirt.

"Dadi, the landlord!" I shout, gasping for breath, my heart thundering against my ribs.

"What is it?" he asks, jumping to the ground.

Mama has been tending the fire to make tea when the sun goes down to break our fast. She sits back on her heels, still as a Buddha tree. She lifts her hands to her face. Auntie stands behind her, wringing her hands, silent for once.

"They're hunting quails by the canal. They're coming for Phulan when they've finished. They're going to take her away!"

"Tell me what they said," says Dadi, taking me by the shoulders and looking into my eyes.

"They say they'll pay. They want her. They saw Mithoo coming here, and the fire was burning." The words tumble out.

Dadi's eyes harden, and suddenly I see the wrestler crouching in the circle of men, muscles bunched and bloodlust in the air.

Gently he sets me aside and walks into the lean-to.

"No!" says Mama, fear shaking in her voice. She stands and Dadi comes out, the old country gun glinting gray and ugly in his hands. "Abassi," she says, her eyes begging. She runs to him and covers his thick hands with her slender brown fingers. "They'll kill you without a thought."

"Nazir Mohammad is very angry," I say quietly, and Dadi and Mama look at me. "I threw water on him."

Phulan looks from my face to Dadi's to Mama's, her fear mounting.

"Stay by the fire," Dadi says to Mama. "Shabanu, you and Phulan help Auntie pack the most important things. Leave what isn't important. Take the dowry, bedding, and food. But keep the fire going." He leaps onto the curve of his camel's neck and tucks the gun under the girth of the saddle. He settles himself behind the camel's hump.

"Where are you going?" asks Mama.

"Hamir will need to know. The landlord knows who we are. If he comes here looking for us and we're not here, he'll look for Hamir next. As soon as you can, head for Derawar."

He looks at me.

"Keep the North Star behind your left shoulder," he says. "Stay off the track. It will be slower, but they can't follow you over the dunes in a jeep. I will catch up with you sometime in the night."

I feel hollow inside. The patterns of my life—the one I have known, the changes I was beginning to accept—shift, and the pieces turn in a swirling nightmare of patches that won't fit together. But there is not time to think now. I am grateful to know exactly what to do.

Mama kneels by the fire in case they watch from a distance. It is still light enough that they can see her yellow *chadr*. A gun fires, and another. Mama stops in midmotion, terror in her eyes.

"They're hunting. We still have time," I tell her. Four more reports sound.

Behind our camp we strap saddles and bedding, food and cooking pots, our one goatskin of water, and bundles of fodder onto the camels. It's their dinnertime, and they roar in protest. I can feel the eyes of four men straining on our camp from near the canal, where they will be looking for fallen birds. We have just minutes to get away.

We leave the camels and sheep to Sher Dil, who seems to sense the emergency. He runs in large circles, barking and gathering the animals closer together. The females nudge the babies toward the inside, and soon they are in one group, alert and ready to move through the dust rising from their feet.

The panniers are padded, and within minutes we are ready, Auntie and the boys on one camel. Phulan mounts the second.

Slowly I approach the fire, and Mama and I duck into the lean-to. We cut through the wall on the other side and race to the camels. Mama climbs into the pannier with Phulan, and I leap onto Xhush Dil's back, twining my fingers into the long, coarse curls on the top of his powerful hump.

"Uuussshhshshsh," I hiss through clenched teeth. We have removed their bells and bracelets, and I am proud that our great brave camels rise so quickly and silently. A rush of exhilaration makes me shiver; my fear has turned to excitement. I am clearheaded as we sail silently, but for the thump of our pots against the camels' sides, into the desert.

Spin Gul

The blood races through the veins in my throat. I want
to shout with joy, feeling Xhush Dil's powerful shoulders
pump his legs against the hard-packed clay track into the
desert. The sun is gone, and I search for the place where
the dunes make looming gray shadows against the green
and darkening sky, where we can leave the track behind.

One star winks palely, then another, and we sail between the dunes, our *chadr*s flying, the camels breathing

hard. Sher Dil and the herd follow behind, the distance widening between us.

When we have been running the camels hard for an hour, we slow the pace. The sky is bright now, and the sand twinkles under the camels' feet like the stars lighting our way. The North Star perches on my left shoulder, just where Dadi said it should be. The bells of the herd have been too distant to hear for some time now, but suddenly a single bell jangles wildly behind us, and a panicked bleating becomes louder and louder. Mithoo has bolted from the herd and struggles toward us in the cooling desert night.

Phulan sobs, her teeth chattering and shoulders shaking. She cradles her head in her arms, which are braced against the back-and-forth and side-to-side rocking of the pannier, where she sits beside Mama.

"Don't worry," Mama tells her as I pull Xhush Dil back to walk beside their camel. "They won't come after us." Mama strokes Phulan's hair.

"Can you imagine Nazir Mohammad putting his plump backside on a camel?" I ask, trying to make her laugh.

"As long as we stay off the track, they'll never find us," Mama says, stroking Phulan gently.

"The wedding," Phulan gasps between sobs. "It's ruined. We'll never be able to go back."

She may be right. Nazir's pride has been wounded badly, and it is unlikely he will let us get away without taking revenge.

Mama puts her arms around Phulan's quivering shoulders.

"We did the only thing we could do," Mama says. "Dadi and Hamir will find some way to appease him."

But I wonder. *Shutr keena,* camel vengeance. It is the way of camels and men of the desert. The price will be heavy.

By now Mithoo has caught up with us, gasping and snorting, his eyes slipping wildly from side to side, showing white. I call softly to him and he falls into step beside Xhush Dil, taking up the stride of the large camel—a fast walk, his long legs lifting us up and over the dunes that shine silver in the starlight. A sliver of new moon rises like hope on the horizon before us. Mithoo's stride is growing long and adult. He seldom nurses from the milk bag and willingly carries a blanket and water jar. But he is still half infant, half adolescent.

We hold steady at this long striding walk so Dadi can catch up with us. I worry that he'll have been followed, that the landlord's men will catch him before he gets away, or that they'll go straight to Hamir and Murad to exact a price on the spot. My heart grows heavier the more I think about it.

After another hour a more immediate problem is apparent. We have only one goatskin of water, and it could be dangerous for us to go to the well at Derawar. The boys are crying for water, but I'm afraid to stop yet to rest.

"Auntie is thirsty too, little ones," Mama tells them. "We must be brave and wait for another hour to stop. Then we will all have water and *chapatis*."

Phulan is still crying, her head bent into her arms. Mama kneels in the pannier and lifts Phulan's face, wiping her tears with the edge of her *chadr*.

"What will happen to Sakina and Kulsum and Bibi Lal?" Phulan wails. I haven't thought of them. "And Sharma and Fatima?"

"Sharma and Fatima can take care of themselves," Mama tells her. The confidence in her voice is real. "Hamir and Murad will work out something. Dadi will reach us soon. Don't worry. We must be strong and ready to do anything they say."

Phulan seems to take heart, and we settle down to the long, loping walk of the camels, waiting for Dadi to catch up with us.

The boys fall asleep, and the hours pass in near silence. Phulan is calm, perhaps sleeping.

The crabbed pattern of the stars of Cancer are high overhead, and the nights are growing shorter. At the fast clip we were moving when we started it would have taken just six hours to reach Derawar from Mehrabpur, but at this slower pace perhaps it will take longer. Dadi should have caught up with us an hour after we slowed to a walk.

If he hasn't appeared before we reach Derawar, we will stop and make a camp among the dunes outside the village, and I can watch the well to see if Nazir Mohammad is waiting there with his jeep and his guns. I relax some.

I think of Sher Dil behind us, still a puppy, his body not yet grown into his broad shoulders, thick legs, and floppy ears, entrusted with our entire herd of camels and sheep. Sher Dil, the lion heart. He could not have been better named.

Our pace slows as the hours turn toward dawn, the faintest pewter line broadening on the horizon as the stars slowly dim and leave the sky as they entered it, one by one.

I must have fallen asleep, for my fingers tingle, twined tightly in the hair on Xhush Dil's massive hump, my cheek resting against my arm. We should be close to Derawar, but I can't tell how long we've been going so slowly.

A shot rings out across the desert. We are out of the dunes now, and the sound is clear and sends my heart into my throat, where it sits like a toad threatening to choke me. The camels stop as if they are one beast, and turn in the direction from which the rifle shot came, their heads high, nostrils flexing, ears swiveling. We all sit upright, silent and watching.

I whirl Xhush Dil in a narrow turn, finding the North Star where it has fallen near the horizon, and head straight toward it, leaving Derawar off to our right.

The camels hit full stride willingly, but they tire quickly, and within ten minutes a dozen camels with uniformed riders pull up beside us.

"Ho, sister," says their leader, taking Xhush Dil's reins. "I didn't mean to frighten you." They are Desert Rangers. The toad in my throat disappears. I want to weep with relief and exhaustion.

"I am *Subadar* Spin Gul. I have a message from Dalil Abassi, sent by the Ranger post at Maujgarh. Is Abassi head of this family?" Mama nods.

"Then he orders you to return to Mehrabpur at once."

"How can that be?" asks Mama. Our tired camels stand, heads lowered, breathing heavily. "My husband was to join us at Derawar."

"We've just come from there to tell you he wants you to go to Mehrabpur. He says to tell you the trouble is past, and it is safe for you to return."

"I don't believe it," says Mama. "He knows I wouldn't believe it, and he would come himself. Please radio back to Maujgarh and ask them to describe the man who called himself Abassi."

The *subadar* shrugs his shoulders in exasperation.

"Sister, the radio is for official use."

"The landlord Nazir from Mehrabpur tried to kidnap and rape my daughters," Mama says, her eyes flashing. "And if that's how you treat me, don't call me sister!"

"I'm sorry," says *Subadar* Spin Gul. "We can't get involved in family feuds."

"We barely escaped with our lives! My husband was due to meet us at Derawar long before now. We never intended to go to Maujgarh. Nazir may have thought we would go there, as it's closer. We are Cholistanis. The Rangers have always protected us."

"I see," says the *subadar*. He turns and issues orders to his men. "We will stay here with you and see that no harm comes to you," he says. "We should have an answer back within two hours. For now you look as if you could do with some tea and food."

Mama and I exchange looks, and it is agreed. We will put ourselves in the care of the Rangers.

"Uuuushshshshh," I say, and Xhush Dil bends his great shaggy head, his front knees folding under him, then his back legs, and he settles with a quiet, grateful groan. My cousins are still sleeping, and Mama and Phulan take one boy each in their arms while I spread blankets on the ground for them to lie upon. I go back to help Auntie out of her pannier. In the gathering light her face is pale.

"Are you unwell?" I ask. She doesn't reply but leans heavily on my shoulder as I help her to the quilts where her sleeping sons lie. She turns her back to me and lies curled on her side. Auntie must be very ill indeed if she is unable to complain.

Subadar Spin Gul and his men unroll tents for us— canvas tents with side walls and windows and ropes. One man has built a fire and is making tea. Another mixes flour and water for *chapati*s. I am so grateful, the toad threatens to leap into my throat again and prevent me from speaking, and tears burn behind my eyes.

Mama and Phulan unload the camels, leaving the saddles and cooking pots tied in place in case we should have to move again.

"You must rest here for the day," says Spin Gul. "Your animals have been driven hard, and you need water," he says, pointing to our single goatskin. Full when we left, it is flat as a *chapati* now. I gasp. What trouble we'd be in if they hadn't found us!

Subadar Spin Gul goes to the camel to which the goat-skin is tied and lifts it in the air. The sun peeps over the edge of the horizon, and a tiny golden drop slips out of one corner of the skin, which has grown dark with wet-ness.

"It will be easy to fix, and I think we can give you another," he says, handing it to one of his men, who reaches into a sack on his belt and picks out a tiny piece of bitumen. He jams it in the fork of a stick and holds it in the fire until a thread of black pitch melts down. Skill-fully he applies the gooey end of the stick to the wet-stained corner. He holds the corner above the fire, letting the heat dry the skin and the pitch penetrate the broken place. He then goes to the side of one of the Rangers' camels, lifts down a square tin, and pours several cups of water into the skin. He hands it back to Spin Gul, who holds it up to the light again. After several seconds there still are no drips.

"Good as new," he says, and for the first time I notice how like Dadi's face his is, kind and handsome and strong in the golden sunlight that spreads its warmth across the flat desert. I could cry for his kindness, and suddenly I am very tired. But it's as if a taut wire stretches through me, through my head from ear to ear, down my neck, across my shoulders, down my spine, and into my legs. I won't be able to sleep until we've learned what's happened to Dadi.

I have a vision of Dadi wounded and fallen, his camel having lost its way. I am working up the courage to ask the *subadar* if he might send a man along the way we've come—a tracker could follow our way easily—in case Dadi is lying in the desert.

Spin Gul's eyes lift, and I turn to look back toward the way we've come. A cloud of dust shimmers, reflecting light from the rising sun as two camels race toward us.

It is Dadi and another man—Hamir? I can't tell, except that he is tall and broad-shouldered, with a mustache and a straight back.

Before the camels reach us, Dadi jumps to the ground and stumbles forward into the arms of the *subadar*. Mama gasps. Dadi's tunic is covered with blood, newly soaked through, still red but dry. I look up at the young man, who steps on the *U* of his camel's neck. He wears country slippers, embroidered, with toes that curl up in a long slender strip. They slap as he jumps lightly to the ground. The camels' sides heave and their heads hang low. A wheezing sound comes from their chests.

The young man also has blood over the front of his tunic, and his hands, too, are stained red. Neither he nor

Dadi seems hurt. Both camels have broad country guns stuck under their girths. They look as if they have run full speed from Mehrabpur and are about to drop.

With a start I realize the young man is Murad. Tired as I am and sick with worry and fear, anxious as I am to know what has happened, I feel the odd turning in my belly again.

"Where is he?" asks Phulan, her voice bright with fear as she looks behind them for another camel carrying Hamir.

"Someone had to stay," Murad says. His eyes are gentle and serious. He is very tall, with hands as broad as a camel's foot, a strong neck, and a square chin with a deep cleft just in the center. I've never seen anyone more handsome.

"Whose blood?" asks Mama, pointing at their tunics, her hand open and flat. Dadi and Murad exchange a long look.

"Hamir's," says Dadi, still breathing heavily.

"What's happened?" shrieks Phulan, throwing herself at Dadi. He puts his arms around her.

"Hamir is dead," he says. Phulan sinks against him, sobbing, and he holds her for several minutes. Mama leads Phulan to the tent. Her face is frozen, mouth open in a silent, anguished cry.

Spin Gul takes Dadi and Murad away to wash, and Dadi tells me to walk their still-wheezing camels until they are cool and breathe normally.

I mourn for Phulan, then pleasure at seeing Murad steals

into my heart like a guilty secret. He has grown fully into his ears. I look under the camels' necks as I walk them, and I watch Murad wash from Spin Gul's goatskin. He has removed his turban and tunic, and the early sunlight sparkles on the smooth brown skin of his broad shoulders.

The men leave us women to rest and grieve in the tent through the morning.

Phulan sits in the back doorway of the tent, away from where the men tend the camels and smoke cigarettes. She keens softly at first, her voice rising to a wail, then trailing off into exhaustion. She raises her arms and throws back her head with another primeval wail.

"God, my life was perfect, and you struck him down. Just when I'm happy, everything changes!" she says to the sky.

Spin Gul returns to tell us that Dadi has been on the radio with the Rangers at Yazman.

"The man who called himself Abassi at Yazman was fat and wore a silk tunic over muddy trousers," Spin Gul tells Mama. "The Rangers at Yazman have taken Murad's family under protection. They are trying to find Nazir Mohammad to negotiate a truce. His older brother, a landowner called Rahim, is a politician and doesn't want trouble. Perhaps he will help."

Rahim—"the merciful." If he is well named, perhaps he will guarantee our safety and we will go to Yazman for the men to talk with the landlords.

Near lunchtime Auntie moans with pain. All morning

she has lain motionless and, except for an occasional groan, silent. It is most unlike her. The boys have gone outside to look for Sher Dil, who should appear with the herd sometime early in the afternoon. He will have taken his time, for there are dozens of babies who must rest on the long trek from Mehrabpur.

Mama first notices the stain of red on the quilt and calls me to her. Auntie is aborting her fetus, and there is little we can do. Mama sends me to the village near Derawar, to the unfriendly people who refused to help find a place to bury Grandfather, who spilled his blood for them. I am to find a midwife to ease Auntie's pain, perhaps to save her unborn baby.

Xhush Dil rises stiffly to his feet, but like a soldier who knows his duty, he heads straight to the village. Dadi and Murad sit inside the Ranger post on a string cot; they wait in silence, their hands folded in front of them. Spin Gul comes out, Dadi behind him. Spin Gul directs me to the midwife's hut.

"Isn't there a doctor?" Dadi asks.

Spin Gul shakes his head.

Dadi leaps up behind me onto Xhush Dil's back. There is an odd, musty smell about him that I know instinctively as the smell of the blood on his tunic. We ride to the midwife's house, and I am grateful to see our friend Shahzada in the doorway, his tattered red fez perched sideways on his shiny brown skull.

"Abassi-*sahib*!" he says, pleasure lighting his crinkled old eyes as he greets Dadi.

"Shahzada, we need your help again," Dadi says with sadness. "I should be bringing a gift to show our gratitude for your kindness when my father died. Instead I come with another problem."

"We are brothers," says Shahzada. "Your time to repay kindness will come in the next life, if not in this."

The midwife is Shahzada's sister, only slightly younger, with the same kindness and the same three long teeth as those of her brother. She listens silently as I describe Auntie's condition, then ducks back into her mud house to grab a bag of herbs and powders. She climbs up on Xhush Dil and we hurry back to the tent, where Auntie lies now on her back, in a widening stain of blood, her eyes rolled back into her head.

Phulan still keens outside the back door of the tent, and I go out to keep the boys company in their vigil for Sher Dil and the herd. I pull them up onto Xhush Dil's hump behind me, and they squirm and giggle as the great camel lurches once again to his feet.

We walk slowly, for the sun is high, and though the clouds still dull its heat, the air is heavy; its weight seems to add to the burdens on my soul.

When we return, Auntie sleeps peacefully on a clean quilt, dressed in her green silk tunic. Shahzada, his sister the midwife, and Dadi are gone, and it is as if nothing has happened at all, except for the small shrouded bundle in the corner of the tent.

"It was another boy," Mama whispers, and she takes me with her to bury it like a piece of excrement in the sand.

Yazman

The next morning we awake to a rumbling sky. A good omen, perhaps, that the rain will come and wash away the pain of death and fill the *toba*s so we can go home after the wedding?

The wedding! There will be no wedding. Again, the dislocated bits of our lives swirl. I try to roll over, to pretend I am dreaming, but I hear men talking outside the tent.

The tent doors are tied shut. Phulan lies on a quilt,

arms outstretched, her silken hair a tangle of black around her anguished, pale face. In the gray light that filters through the tent from the stormy sky outside she looks dead, but I know the look of a grieving woman.

I go outside, where Auntie is up and clucking about her sons as if nothing has happened to her. How strange life is; it's all there is, for now at least, yet to some it seems to have so little meaning.

Tea and *chapatis* are waiting, and I go to the fire where Mama turns the flat round bread fresh off the pan. I am hungry.

Mama's eyes have a white tightness around them, and her mouth is set in a straight, thin line. She doesn't look up as I squat across the fire from her.

Dadi and Murad, their tunics and *lungis* clean but still stained with dull, rusty blood marks, lean against the kneeling camels. They have deep shadows of beard on their chins. Their eyes are red-rimmed with lack of sleep. They do not talk, just lean, arms folded across their chests, looking at the fire.

The rain starts falling in fat plops that signal we are in for a day of wet weather—lifesaving, inconvenient, glorious, wet, cool, blessed water.

Dadi and Murad stay where they are as Mama and I scurry to tie a shelter to the tent cords to cover the fire, and pull our things inside. They are so engrossed, staring and waiting, that they barely notice the now pelting water. Instinctively my heart lifts. Rain does that to desert people, and I am still giddy from seeing Murad. But the truth is that the sky is crying for Hamir, for Phulan, perhaps for all of us.

"What are Dadi and Murad waiting for?" I ask Mama. I can't stand this pained silence.

"Word of when we have to return to pay for all this foolishness you've caused," says Auntie. Her face is pale, and though her face and hands are still plump, she looks smaller, as though the loss of this baby has diminished her.

I am speechless at her insensitivity, but I remind myself that she had to hide her hurt when she was young and her sisters and cousins were married off one at a time while she grew fatter and fatter; and now with the loss of her tiny, unformed baby—I manage to ignore her suggestion that I have caused this situation.

"What will happen, Mama?" I ask quietly, reasonably, forcing her to look me in the eye as we squat across from each other, the fire between us.

"We'll see, Shabanu, we'll see," she answers. Then she looks away; she knows it's not enough of an answer. "Dadi and Murad have been on the Rangers' radio all night. On the other end in Yazman was the landlord Rahim-*sahib*. He and the Rangers guarantee our safety. He says the death of Hamir has appeased his brother. He won't let Nazir harm us."

"Why?" I ask quietly.

She sighs and pokes a stick into the fire.

"What does it matter, Shabanu?"

"Because what he wants of us matters!" I cry.

176

"Rahim-*sahib* is a politician," Mama answers wearily. She too has been up all night, listening to the men talk on the radio. "Nazir Mohammad threatens to take Murad's land and cut off his water, to turn it back into desert—out of spite. A councilman wouldn't want his constituents to know he had a brother like that."

"Thank God for pride and greed," I say, and Mama gives me a sharp look.

"What does he want in return?" I ask again, for I know nothing comes without its price.

"That's what we're waiting to hear," she says. "Go get your father and Murad to come in out of the rain. They've lost the sense God gave them at birth."

They are only a few feet away, but my tunic is soaked through by the time I am close enough for them to hear me. I can't look Murad in the face, but I take Dadi's hand.

"You can't help any of us if you die of wet and cold," I say. I feel Murad's look on my face, and it burns under the cool rain water. Dadi puts an arm across my shoulders, and the two follow me under the shelter like old men shuffling to their graves.

Spin Gul rides up, water dripping in rivulets from his rain cape, the fur on his camel's neck matted and clumped. He orders the camel to kneel, and his weariness too is apparent from the way he moves slowly, as if double weights have been added to his arms and legs.

"When the rain stops we should start out. Probably by tomorrow morning," he says, accepting a cup of sweetened milk tea. Dadi and Murad are standing, but Spin

Gul squats beside the fire. "Rahim-*sahib* has shamed his ass of a brother. They have agreed to meet you at Yazman. We will accompany you to Dingarh. The Rangers at Dingarh will take you straight to the post at Yazman. The landlords will meet you there."

Murad paces, and Dadi stares into the fire a moment before answering.

"Is that all? What of Murad's family?"

"Rahim-*sahib* said he wants nothing in return. Just peace in his constituency. He offered to protect Murad's family personally, but they will stay with the Rangers until things are settled and they can return home."

The day is endless. Phulan sleeps most of it, and when she wakes, she is staring and silent. I know she is in pain. I have thought of Murad as a husband just this one day. I don't know where the joy has come from amid this pain and confusion. But Phulan has aimed her entire existence at marrying Hamir. Her life has come to a sudden stop. I pity her, but I can't help wanting to shake her, to tell her to wake up and prepare for what comes next.

I fear Nazir will want her; that will be the price of freedom for the rest of us, peace for Murad's family and water for his land. I doubt she has thought that far ahead, but if she has, it's reason enough to grieve. Again a vision of Nazir Mohammad's fat flesh wobbling as he sweats over my beautiful sister sends a shiver of revulsion through me.

The rain ends late in the afternoon, and pools of water surround us. Sher Dil paws and barks at the water. The camels drink deeply; it is the first time they have had sweet water in the two months since the sandstorm dried up our *toba*. Mithoo gallops through the water, splashing up great silver sheets and frightening the other young camels.

I try to get Phulan to look at the magical sunset, hoping the great opal haze will soothe her. But she is immobile, and I sit with her at the edge of a dune.

Mama, Dadi, and Murad have spent the afternoon resting, and they come out to check the gear and count the herd before the sun goes down. I watch Murad's wide shoulders, his strong hands probing gently at a tender spot on the leg of a lame camel. The thought of marrying him brings immeasurable joy and fear to my heart. Phulan's joy has turned to dust, and it has taught me a lesson about the fragility of happiness.

We sleep little in the night, all of us thinking about the consequences of Nazir Mohammad's fury and whether his brother Rahim-*sahib* will be able to negotiate a settlement. It's difficult to imagine that the greedy, spoiled man in the silk trousers will let the indignity he suffered pass. The life of a peasant farmer may not be enough payment.

We are up and moving about, filling our goatskins and loading camels before the stars have left the sky. When the Rangers come for us we have been waiting nearly two hours, ready to leave.

Phulan takes some milk tea, the first time in two days she has drunk or eaten. The skin under her eyes is bruised from crying. But she seems more alert and answers Mama's questions about how she feels.

"Empty," says Phulan. "As if nothing inside me or outside is worth caring about."

"You have so much to care about," says Mama, stroking Phulan's pale forehead. "You have Dadi and Shabanu and me, all of your cousins and aunts and uncles who love you. We will make another marriage for you."

"It was so perfect. He was more than most girls can expect to marry. And Shabanu would be with us in another year, and we would always be together. Now I'm afraid. I don't know what will happen."

"We won't let anything bad happen to you, daughter," says Mama. Dadi has been standing with his back to them, adjusting straps and balancing the loads, distributing them so that the stronger camels carry more, the females and smaller males less. He says nothing, just turns away to another camel.

Five Rangers accompany us to Dingarh, all of them armed and watchful. They are men of the desert and ride their camels as if they are part of the animals. None of them speak, and we are quiet as the sun rises higher in the sky, heating the day like an oven fired for bread, the water coming out of the sand in steamy shimmers.

We reach Dingarh, where another group of Rangers comes forward on camels. They salute our escorts, who turn without stopping for food and water and head back toward Derawar.

We have made the trip in ten hours—good time, considering we walked slowly enough for the herd to keep up with us. One of the Rangers rides ahead to the Wing

Command mess to fetch Murad's nephew, who will stay with Sher Dil and the herd while we go into Yazman. We walk the rest of the way into town, the Rangers making a protective ring around us.

We go straight to the Wing Command headquarters, where Colonel Haq greets the other Rangers with a smart salute. Without getting down or giving us a chance to thank them properly, the Rangers turn their camels and head back through town toward Dingarh. Everyone is very solemn.

Colonel Haq shows Dadi and Murad to a room next to his office where they will wait for the landlords to arrive. He orders a young captain to show us to the quarters where Bibi Lal, Kulsum, and little Sakina have slept since Hamir died and we fled into the desert. Suddenly it occurs to me they may blame us for Hamir's death.

We are shown to a room that adjoins Bibi Lal's, and Mama knocks on her door. Kulsum opens it and embraces Mama, a long, full embrace of shared sadness.

"Oh, sister, God will protect us," she says softly, holding Mama at arm's length.

"Come in, come in," says Bibi Lal, sitting on the floor feeding one of her grandchildren from a tin cup. The furrows of grief on her face are deep, but she is calm and purposeful. "We have as much to discuss as the men do."

She wipes the child's chin and sends her with Sakina and the other children into our room, shutting the door between us.

Phulan lies with her back to us on one of the string

cots, and Sakina stands tentatively by the door, biting her lips, her small niece straddling one hip. She wears a blue faded tunic and skirt that have grown too short above her brown bare feet. She reminds me of myself just six months ago.

"Come in, Sakina, come sit beside me," I say. She sits down on the cot shyly and lifts her little niece up to her shoulder. Her nephew bangs a stick against the wooden leg of the cot. Auntie's boys start banging cups against the floor. I send the three little boys outside with strict orders to stay by the door, which I leave open so I can keep an eye on them.

I feel very awkward as I sit down again beside Sakina, who adored her older brother Hamir, as I'm sure I would have adored an older brother.

"I'm so sorry about Hamir," I blurt out, not knowing what to say. Phulan sits up on her cot and gathers her *chadr* around her.

"How did it happen?" Phulan asks. Sakina remains silent, her lips pressed between her teeth and looking at the floor.

"You don't have to tell," I say.

"Yes, she does!" Phulan says, showing some life for the first time in three days. "I want to know what happened."

"Uncle Abassi came riding fast on his camel," Sakina begins, her voice barely a whisper. She hugs the child closer to her. "He told us Nazir Mohammad was going to kidnap Phulan," she says, looking up for the first time.

"He said 'They're going to give Phulan to the man who shoots the most quails, and probably Shabanu will be passed around them.' He said they might even come for me." Her voice grows stronger, and she bends to set her sleeping niece down on the cot, covering her with a shawl.

"He said you had gone into the desert, and he thought you'd be safe. But he was worried about us.

"Before we could decide what to do, Hamir stood up, as if he was going outside to relieve himself. Then he turned in the doorway and came back and got his gun. Uncle Abassi and Murad asked him where he was going with the gun. But Hamir was angry and he started shouting. Uncle tried to take the gun away, but Hamir aimed it at him.

"Hamir was like a wild man. He always had a terrible temper, and he took offense easily. He told them they didn't know how to act like men, that the landlord had insulted the woman he was going to marry and his uncle and brother were acting like cowards. Then Uncle said they should go outside."

Sakina stops for a breath. Phulan sits transfixed, and I get up to pour Sakina a cup of water. She takes a sip and goes on.

"Murad told Kulsum and me to begin packing some things, and that we should follow you into the desert. He and Hamir would come with us to Derawar. Uncle would go straight to Yazman to get help from the Rangers. Uncle said the police superintendent wouldn't be power-ful enough to stand up to Nazir Mohammad because he has two other brothers, including Rahim-*sahib*, who is a member of the district council.

"Uncle and Hamir were outside, and Hamir was shouting at Uncle that he was a coward. My mother went to the door to beg him to be sensible. She didn't want him to be shot. Hamir said Nazir Mohammad would steal our land if we went away. She and Uncle tried to talk to him.

"But the more they talked, the crazier Hamir got, and he threatened to kill Uncle. I think they were going to fight, but suddenly we heard a jeep, and we knew Nazir was coming after us.

"It was after dark. We saw the lights coming from a long distance. Murad hurried us up and put us on the camels. He told us to ride straight for Yazman to the Desert Rangers Wing Command. I knew where to come. We deliver milk to them."

"Did you go straight away?" asks Phulan, pressing for every detail.

"We started out, and then a second jeep came from the other direction. The men in the jeep saw us in their lights. Murad had disappeared, so we turned back toward the house. I think the men were drunk. They were shouting, and we couldn't understand their words. The fat landlord said something like 'Hamir, bring us your sister!' and then there was a gunshot and shouting and confusion, then another gunshot, much louder than the first."

She sits and thinks for a moment.

"Go on, go on!" Phulan says.

"I think the first shot was Hamir's and the second was

one of Nazir Mohammad's men. Nazir was too drunk to shoot a gun straight. My mother got down from her camel and she saw the whole thing. After the second shot, Hamir flew off his feet and never moved again. The blood was everywhere. It almost cut him in half and . . ."

"Oh, God! Oh, God!" Phulan cries, and buries her face in her hands.

"What happened then?" I ask.

"People were running in all directions. The men got back into their jeeps and drove away, their wheels skidding in the sand. We got down from our camels, and Uncle Abassi and Murad carried Hamir inside. We washed him quickly and buried him inside the house, all of us saying prayers at once. We were afraid they'd come back. Your father insisted it would be safer for us to stay at Yazman, and he and Murad came after you. That's all. You know the rest."

We have been so transfixed that I have forgotten all about my cousins until I hear them shrieking. I run to the doorway. They have put a ladder up to the mango tree by the colonel's office door, and it has fallen after they have climbed into the branches.

"Wait, don't move!" I shout, and run out to pick up the ladder. As I hold it steady, I hear a car in the driveway. Oh, Dadi will kill me if I'm out here with the boys when Nazir comes.

But I can't help it. The boys are terrified, and I am afraid they'll fall or try to jump from the branch. I prop the ladder again, its feet in the mud at the base of the tree, and climb to the branch they cling to and coax them to come down. The car stops, and a door opens and closes. I don't dare turn around. I feel the ladder slipping away from the tree, its feet unsteady in the mud.

I hold my arms around the boys and cling to the tree and ladder when suddenly the slipping stops.

"Just hand one boy down at a time," says a calm, deep voice. I look down, and a man about Dadi's age, perhaps older, holds the foot of the ladder.

I take Kulsum's son first, as he is heaviest and least frightened. I tell my cousins to hold tight to the limb while I hand the first boy down to the man at the foot of the ladder. Then I hand down the older of my two cousins and finally climb to the bottom with my smallest cousin on my hip.

"Thank you," I say, looking into the man's face. He has kind eyes with a twinkle in them. His hair is gray around his ears, and he is clean-shaven.

"Young ladies shouldn't be climbing trees," he says.

"I wasn't . . ." I begin, then I realize he's joking, and we laugh.

"Most country girls cover their mouths when they laugh," he says, still joking.

"I have perfect teeth. Why should I cover them?" I bare my teeth for him to see, and he laughs again. I thank him and take my protesting cousins back to our room.

Justice

The men talk late into the night and start again early the next morning. The day seems endless. Around dusk Mama comes from the room where she has sat with Kulsum, Auntie, and Bibi Lal. The children are sleeping, and I ask what we will eat.

"The colonel is sending food. Don't worry," she says.

"Mama, what are you talking about in there?" I ask. "If it concerns Phulan, shouldn't she be with you?"

187

"Shabanu, really. What we decide for both of you is what you will do. You aren't old enough to know what's good for you."

"What about me?" Mama's eyes have a strange look about them again. "I'm talking about Phulan. What is it? What does this have to do with me?" Panic rises inside me.

"Never mind," says Mama, turning to go back to the other room.

"Mama!" But she has closed the door firmly, and the bolt slips into place on the other side before I can push it open again.

Phulan is sleeping on her stomach on the string cot. Sakina sits wide-eyed on the bed. I run to Phulan and shake her shoulder.

"They're deciding something," I say into her ear. "Come with me—I want to know!"

"I don't care what happens," Phulan says from under the canopy her hair makes on the pillow.

"Phulan, you must! They're making plans. For both of us. Come on!" I shake her hard.

"Leave me alone!"

I run outside, but no one is about. The door to the room where the men talk is closed. The guards stand smartly at attention in the courtyard at the front of the Wing Command headquarters, their red, fanned turbans sharp in the glimmering light.

I run around to the window of the room where the

women sit talking. I peer in. Bibi Lal looks up and sees me. I put my hands against the glass and press my face between them.

"Please, let me in," I say, near tears with frustration and fear.

Kulsum comes to the door and opens it a crack.

"Shabanu, please be patient."

I push the door open and brush Kulsum aside.

"If you are talking about me, I want to know what you're saying." I look Mama in the eye.

"Shabanu, you are a child," she says. "Phulan didn't have a say . . ."

"I am not Phulan! I want to know what's going to happen to me. I'll sit here quietly and listen, that's all." Mama cocks her head and lifts an eyebrow. "I promise."

Bibi Lal shifts her large frame aside and pats the rug beside her.

"Everything major is decided anyway," she says. "We should get Phulan then, too." Mama nods, and I sit in the warm circle women always make, fearful of their decision.

Auntie has been sitting quietly, slightly behind Mama, just at the edge of the circle of women. Her silence is the only thing that gives me hope. If the decision is one that works out well for all of us, she will be jealous and discontented. If it is not, she will crow and try to make me feel ashamed and responsible for the bad things that have happened.

Kulsum unbolts the door and goes to fetch Phulan.

"Go away. Leave me alone!" we hear from the other room.

Mama stands stiffly and goes into the next room. She murmurs softly to Phulan for some time.

There's a knock at the outside door, and I nearly jump out of my skin. I am on my feet before anyone else has even looked up. It's our captain with two kerosene lamps, one for each room. I put one on the window sill and the other on the mantel over the empty fireplace. I sense by the way everyone keeps silent that I won't like what will be said.

Phulan comes through the doorway, combing her hair away from her face with her long fingers. She is thinner and paler, but her face is more relaxed and rested. She looks lovely again.

When we are all seated in the circle, the boys playing noisily in one corner of the room, Bibi Lal speaks.

"We have conferred with your father," she says, looking from Phulan to me. "It is agreed that the wedding will be held as planned after forty days of mourning for Hamir, may his soul rest in peace."

In the brief moment of silence that follows, I wonder if one of us is to be married to the Holy Koran, as some girls are, so that there's no question of sharing the land. Dadi wouldn't do that to Phulan or me, I'm sure of it!

"Phulan will marry Murad. He is old enough and ready to be married. He will be a good husband to her."

He was meant for me, I want to shout. Phulan's husband was Hamir! He was just like her, and Murad is like me. We are meant for each other. My ears burn and my throat tightens, but I sit perfectly still, staring at my hands folded in my lap. I can't look at Phulan, who also sits perfectly still.

"Nazir Mohammad has agreed that Murad shall keep all of our land, and he promises not to disturb the flow of irrigation water." Phulan breathes a sigh of relief. I feel ill.

"His elder brother Rahim-*sahib* has asked for Shabanu."

"No!" I say softly at first. "No! No!" Mama and Phulan take me into their arms. I fight them. "I won't do it!"

"Shabanu, Shabanu," says Bibi Lal, leaning forward and taking my face between her huge hands. "He's a decent man, and he's very wealthy. He's a *syed,* and a marriage with him is a great honor for both of our families." A *syed* is a religious leader who traces his lineage back to the family of the Prophet Mohammad. But Rahim-*sahib* is not Murad, *syed* or not.

"How many wives does he have?" I ask, my chin thrust forward.

"Three," Mama replies. "But you will be the youngest by nearly twenty years. You will be the last and always his favorite. He will provide well for you and your sons."

"How old is he?"

"He's only fifty or fifty-five," Mama says.

"He's old enough to be my grandfather!" I say, too

angry now even for tears. "I can't, Mama. How can you do this to me? You can't make me."

"Shabanu, you are still young. You aren't even of age yet. You have another six months, perhaps a year, to get used to the idea." Mama strokes my hair, and Phulan kneels by my side, holding my hand. I pull away from them.

"I'll never get used to marrying a man old enough to be my grandfather. Is he the man who came in the car and held the ladder?"

"Yes," Kulsum says, a twinkle in her eye. "I think he's quite good-looking. He doesn't look fifty-five."

"If you don't agree, Shabanu, how can we be sure the landlords will keep their word?" Auntie asks. "If we say no to Rahim-*sahib,* it won't be long before his brother starts demanding his payments again, and soon enough he'll turn off the water and the land will be ruined."

What a trap they've laid! Phulan is eldest so she must marry first. She is ripe for marriage. Dadi knows that, and he wants it done quickly. Murad is ready too. Because I am not of age yet, I am to be sacrificed to keep the bargain!

"Shabanu," says Mama, "when Rahim-*sahib* saw you this afternoon, the first thing he did was ask the colonel, 'Who was that beautiful girl outside on the ladder?' Your father was very angry with you for not keeping an eye on the boys and ending up in a tree when Rahim-*sahib* arrived in his car. He was angry enough to beat you.

"But Rahim-*sahib* said, 'No, she's lovely and intelligent. You mustn't spoil her spirit.' Dadi says Rahim-*sahib* only half concentrated on the talk. He kept looking out the window hoping to catch another glimpse of you. He is in love with you already. He will cherish you. We couldn't do better for you with a boy your own age."

"And we'll be close together," says Phulan, her eyes bright. "We can see each other almost every day! Rahim-*sahib*'s house is only a field away from where Murad's land begins."

"A minute ago you were grieving for Hamir!" I say to her. "How can you change like the wind?"

"Of course I grieve for Hamir," Phulan says, looking down at our hands twined in her lap. "But it's such a good solution! Who knows what might have happened to you if Rahim-*sahib* hadn't offered to marry you?"

I find it difficult to believe that Rahim-*sahib* would find me so lovely. After I bared my teeth at him. What could I have been thinking? He probably saw I was strong, and he wants someone who can work hard.

"I'll go to live with Sharma," I say, and Mama's slap sends my head flying and my eyes reeling.

"Shabanu," she says, her face harder than I've ever seen it before, "you are to say nothing more. It is done."

The Choice

We return on the camels to the edge of the desert near Mehrabpur five days after we fled our lean-tos in the night. The day is cloudy, and the sky churns and rumbles with the threat of rain.

At first we think we've come to the wrong place.

Where our lean-tos had stood there is a small village of neat mud huts, painted all over with camels and birds. Ovens and grain storage cupboards line the joint courtyard, where a small girl bends from the waist, sweeping the sand with a broom of desert twigs. Each house is tall enough to stand up in and broad enough to walk around in, despite the string cots and trunks that line the walls. And beside each door sits a clay pot with red, orange, and yellow flowers in it.

As we approach, a man wearing a mirrored and embroidered vest and a starched turban rides toward us on a fine white stallion that prances and tosses his long silver mane. The man carries a box of tooled rosewood in front of him on a saddle decorated with silver medallions.

Mama, Phulan, Bibi Lal, Kulsum, and Auntie cover their faces as he rides up, and Dadi and Murad urge their camels forward to meet him. The wind blows some of their words in our direction:

"Rahim-*sahib* sends greetings . . ."

"Thank you," says Dadi. "Please send our . . ."

". . . sorrow for . . . hopes your daughter will accept these . . . find your houses comfortable," says the man in the turban. "This is your home whenever . . . the servant girl will stay with you . . ."

I can't hear the rest of Dadi's words. I feel Auntie's eyes sharp on my back, urging me to cover my head and face and to stop eavesdropping so obviously.

The man on the silver-white horse hands Dadi the wooden box and turns. Dadi watches him canter away before he returns to us.

"Rahim-*sahib* built these houses for us to make up for the trouble his brother has caused," Dadi says. "This girl is the daughter of his servant, and she'll stay with us as long . . ."

"A servant!" says Mama.

I bet a hundred rupees she is a spy for the landlords. But I have learned to keep my mouth shut, and I certainly will when the girl is around.

"We don't need a servant," says Auntie. "People like us don't use servants. It's a matter of pride."

The girl stands quietly, the twig broom clasped between her hands, staring at the ground. Her tunic, skirt, and *chadr* are faded but clean, and her hair is pulled back in a clasp. She clearly has been treated well in the landlord's household.

"We'll see," says Dadi. He looks amused, as if he is enjoying Rahim-*sahib*'s efforts to set things right.

"What's in the box?" Auntie asks, forgetting the servant girl.

Dadi orders the camels to their knees, and everyone but me jumps down. Dadi holds the box out to me, but I am immobile.

"How can I accept a gift from him?" I ask quietly. "Is he buying me?"

"Shabanu," says Dadi, his voice stern, his eyes commanding me to come to him. "He already *has* bought you. He has paid more than a fair price for a troublesome girl like you. You may as well get used to the idea. Can't you see he wants you to be happy?"

I cannot move. With all that Rahim-*sahib* has done, I am shocked that he also has paid a bride price! Dadi takes a step toward me, a threat in his eye, and wearily, as if my body is making a great effort to overcome the laws of nature, I get down from Xhush Dil and stand before my father.

Everyone crowds around me, gabbling like crows with excitement. Only Murad stands apart. He takes the camels to the canal for water. Slowly I lift the lid. Inside the red velvet-lined box are gold bangles wrapped in tissue, a diamond nose pin clipped to a piece of felt, and a small velvet sack. Dadi holds the wooden box as I loosen the drawstring and shake the sack. A delicate gold ring set with rubies and emeralds and diamonds tumbles into my palm.

"Put it on!" says Phulan. I look up at her, and her eyes shine with happiness for me. I am miserable. Everyone thinks something magical has happened. And what's on my mind? The fleeting hope that Murad has gone to the canal because he is disturbed that I should have a gift from the landowner.

I tell myself to be realistic. Murad must be delighted to be marrying Phulan. She is so beautiful, and under her silly poses she is kind and will be a good wife. She needs patience and discipline—surely Hamir offered neither.

"Come on, Shabanu, put it on!" she urges, and I slip the exquisite shimmering ring onto my finger. "The bangles, and the nose pin, too!" I oblige mechanically, and they all dance around and tell me how wonderful I look. Dadi pulls out his snuffbox with the mirror on the lid to show me the diamond nose pin. It reflects thousands of pins of colored light. I think vaguely of the blackness in my heart—I am wearing all the light that ever was within me on my nose and finger.

After a while they stop making a fuss over me, and Mama and Phulan go inside the houses and find the belongings we've left behind, plus several trunks filled with wedding presents for Phulan: dishes, platters, pitchers, boxes of spices, crates of mangoes, bowls, shawls. Bibi Lal and Kulsum look on quietly, and I can see their thoughts have turned to their own house, and Hamir buried under the floor.

Because we don't believe in disturbing a body once it's laid to rest, they will build a new house.

"You can stay with us," says Mama. "We will help you, and you will have a house in just a few days. Come on."

But when we get to the farm, there are two new houses, one for Phulan and Murad, the other for Bibi Lal and the rest of the family; both are much grander than ours. They're large and light and well built, and someone has dug a tiny pond behind them for bathing.

Bibi Lal finds her entire household has been replaced in the new house. The old house stands where they had left it in the middle of Murad's farm, with Hamir buried under the floor.

We believe in omens, and it isn't long before word of the good fortune that befell us following Hamir's death has spread around the countryside. The legend expands, and people want to visit the tomb of the boy who died and saved his family's farm and brought wealth to his relatives. They leave us in peace to mourn him, and Bibi Lal and Kulsum and Sakina do that well.

We women go into Bibi Lal's house to pray. Murad goes to the house built for him and Phulan a few feet away to receive a group of village men who have been waiting to pay their condolences.

The mourning, which had been postponed by our flight, begins with the force of held-back emotion.

Bibi Lal enters the house, her back straight, and goes to a corner of the main room. She sits on the floor, ankles crossed, facing the wall. A low moan escapes her, and giving way to her grief, she cries and beats her great chest like a drum, pouring out her anguish as Phulan had, keening and wailing like a madwoman.

Sakina covers her head so no one can see her cry, but she is silent for nearly a week, the only sign of what goes on under her *chadr* an occasional shudder of her thin shoulders. Kulsum weeps softly, for she has grown accustomed to grief.

Mama, Phulan, and I do the cooking and receive the women who come to pay their respects. We go home at night to sleep. Auntie stays in her new house to look after the boys. Her feeling of superiority to Mama, Phulan, and me has fled swiftly with the wealth we have gained, and her remarkable physical diminishment continues. Perhaps she will become prettier as she loses weight. She is beginning to have a waist, and her three chins have reduced to one and a half.

Halfway through the forty-day period of mourning, the wedding preparations begin. We receive word that Uncle will join us, and Auntie seems happy for the first time since I can remember. Sharma and Fatima and other relatives also send word of their arrival. With the three houses Rahim-*sahib* has built, we can have many of them stay with us. The rest stay in lean-tos.

And gradually, as the number of people and activities multiplies, a strange thing happens. Flags begin to appear around the house where Hamir's body lies buried under the floor. Someone brings an inscribed marble slab with the promise of a full tomb after the first anniversary of his death. Word of his heroic death and our resultant wealth spreads wider and wider, like ripples in a pond, and Hamir's house becomes a shrine.

The monsoon rains come and go, usually pouring water on us in the afternoons, cooling the earth briefly. Then the late afternoon sun breaks through the clouds, heating the ground again and sending wisps of steam into the air most of the evening and following morning. It's hot and muggy, except when it rains, and I feel trapped in a torpor that leaves us with little energy other than that required to keep a routine of pampering Phulan.

Auntie worries that Phulan is too thin. She makes special mixtures of yogurt and honey, vegetables and butter and sugar, and spoons them into Phulan's mouth.

"No more, Auntie, please," Phulan says, sighing. She pushes away Auntie's hand, which holds a spoonful of cooked sweet carrot pudding with nuts and raisins, and lies back on a bolster covered with embroidery, a gift from Sakina.

The hollows under Phulan's eyes disappear, and her cheeks and arms round out again. She is like a ripe melon, healthy and lovely and fragrant.

Every morning Mama and I massage jasmine oil sparkling with golden powders—tumeric, cumin, and saffron—into Phulan's skin, which has turned from the paleness of her grief to a glowing copper that shines smoothly around the soft curves of her arms, legs, and face.

At night she weeps when we massage her hair with sandalwood paste and mustard oil. She complains that it burns. In the morning Mama sends me with a jar to fetch water from the canal, and she washes Phulan's hair until her ears are bright pink. Phulan dries it in the sun and wears it like a black silken shawl, spread around her shoulders and down her back.

Phulan has become nearly unbearable, ordering everyone to do things for her.

"Please, Shabanu," she asks sweetly, "bring my scarf. Not the blue one, the green one." The servant girl stays on, unobtrusively at first. She returns to her family at Rahim-*sahib*'s house each night, and we grow used to having her, especially with Phulan's extra demands.

She experiments with makeup. Bibi Lal has given her a sculpted brass vial of golden powder and a pot of rouge. Every morning she lines her eyes with black kohl and massages the soft gold powder into the creases of her lids.

The color softens on her skin, leaving her tiger eyes looking fiery. She wipes it away before Dadi comes home. But
she'll wear it on her wedding day.

Phulan spends her days resting, eating, and sleeping,
being pampered and fussed over, trying on her dowry
clothes and jewelry, and talking about the sons she will
have.

Half of me longs to be Phulan. She will marry my own
dear Murad, and she is beautiful. I am small and strong
with too much spirit, and I think too much. I am lonely
and fearful, and I long for the days when I was free in the
desert.

Again the man on the white horse comes, the starched
pleats of his turban dazzling in the monsoon sunlight. Dadi
holds the reins as the man dismounts. This time he hands
Dadi a tiny sack of lambskin tied with gold threads. Dadi
thanks him, and the man bows formally. Mirrors dazzling
on his vest, he remounts his silver horse and rides away
again.

I untie the threads, and a silver vial with vines and
flowers carved over its surface slides into my palm. I open
the stopper, a tiny dove perched atop a long ivory appli-
cator, and draw out a miniature spoonful of lapis lazuli
powder to decorate my own eyes.

I do resent his trying to buy my heart. Bride price is
common here in the desert—I don't begrudge Mama and
Dadi that. It has insured their future, and they won't have
to worry about drought or anything else ever again. But
my heart. I never knew I had one until I lost Guluband.

Was Guluband's loss destined to prepare me for losing Murad? What will I lose next? Death I understood before. But loss for any other reason has always seemed unnecessary until now.

The night Hamir died seems like a bad dream, unreal but for the fact that he is gone, and I mourn privately for him and for myself, taking Xhush Dil into the desert and stealing as much time as I can to be among the dunes. Mithoo, growing bigger and stronger, comes along, his nose next to my ankle as Xhush Dil walks.

I decide one day to teach Mithoo to dance. I have noticed that when I sing his ears swivel, the way Guluband's used to do. Mithoo has the same desire to dance as Guluband had. I touch the backs of his front legs with a stick and sing to him. Within just a few days he lifts his feet high without prompting whenever I sing. I must get Dadi to buy him bracelets, so he can match the rhythms of his feet to the songs I sing.

My absence is little noticed once I have fed the animals. I take my cousins with me to tend the herd. I savor my limited freedom, perhaps only because I know my days in the desert with my beloved camels are numbered.

Sharma arrives a day late, by the light of a waxing moon. As usual, we hear her long before we see her. Even her animals are noisy, each with a jangling bell tied around its neck. They are fat and healthy, fully recovered from the drought. It's said Sharma has magic—I've heard people talk about her as if she were a witch—but to me her magic is power.

She and Fatima ride an aged female camel, their sheep and goats following behind, and Sharma sings, her voice strong and clear. Mama, Dadi, Phulan, and I come out of our house, where we have been spreading our quilts on the string cots.

The camel kneels without command, and Sharma wraps her arms around Phulan, for she has heard of Hamir's death. Phulan returns Sharma's hug, and when Sharma holds her at arm's length, my clever aunt knows Hamir's passing causes my sister more joy than sorrow.

Mama and Phulan fill Sharma and Fatima in on what has happened in the weeks since we've seen her. I make myself busy at the fire, preparing tea and making *chapati*s for them.

"So, you've paid for all this with your little Shabanu," Sharma says. Dadi, who has been relaxing and smoking his *hookah*—a fancy blue and white ceramic one, a gift from Rahim-*sahib*—sits forward.

"It's a good solution," Dadi says. "It isn't only the money, which I don't deny has helped. But what would have become of Shabanu? There are no other prospects, and we are within months of the time when she should be married."

"How far have you looked?" Sharma spits out the words. Dadi looks wounded, for he too believes in Sharma's magic and considers her a wise woman.

"She could never have done better with a desert boy," says Dadi. "She would be tending camels and children and moving from *toba* to *toba* the rest of her life, never knowing when the rain will stop and the vegetation will dry up. This way she'll have everything."

"Everything! She'll be his fourth wife. He already has seven sons. His youngest wife is still of childbearing age. He's not so rich that he can afford to leave all of them land and houses and money. They all live in one house now. That's difficult for women sharing a single man.

"Shabanu will be their slave. They're all uppity-uppity women. They get along all right. But what about her? Do you think they'll take a desert girl into their circle? And when he dies, the seven sons he has—and perhaps his third wife will bear him one or two more—will inherit his property. There will be nothing for Shabanu and the sons she bears. She'll be a penniless widow by the time she's twenty. And what if she has daughters? They'll marry similarly, unless she's lucky enough to marry them back to the desert!"

"But Rahim-*sahib* is very healthy, and he'll live to be an old man," says Mama.

"Bah!" says Sharma, and they break into a raucous discussion, shouting and interrupting each other.

"There is another consideration, Sharma," says Dadi, his spine stiff. Dadi might allow Mama's eccentric cousin to criticize, but he won't let her change his mind. "Rahim-*sahib*'s marriage to Shabanu will ensure that his greedy brother keeps his hands off Murad's land."

"Aha!" says Sharma. "But why Shabanu? Phulan is more

likely to appeal to a man like Rahim-*sahib,* and knowing
how to keep a man comes naturally to her. You can tell
by the way she walks. . . ."

"Because he wants Shabanu! And that's the end of it."
Dadi stalks out of the house, taking his *hookah* with him.

Long after Phulan and Mama have gone to sleep, Dadi
still has not returned. He listens to Sharma. No matter
how outrageous what she says might be, he knows she
speaks the truth. And he does not want to hurt me.

There's no question of my being able to sleep. When
the moon is highest, I slip out and bathe myself in the
blue-white light of the desert night. I hear the gentle noises
of the camels as they chew their cud, grunt, and belch. I
go to Sharma's house to see if she and Fatima are still
awake.

They talk quietly in the third and last house Rahim-
sahib has built for us.

"Shabanu, how do you feel about this marriage your
father has arranged for you?" she asks.

Fatima lights the lanterns, and Sharma's figure makes a
long, straight shadow. My shadow is half the height of
hers. Sharma sits on the string cot and crosses her ankles
in front of her. Fatima joins her, and I sit on the cot across
from them.

"What can I do?" I ask. "Do you think I want to marry
him? Mama says he's already in love with me. He's sending presents. Look!" I hold out my hand and show the
ring and bangles. Sharma whistles through her teeth.

"Don't be taken in by it," she says. "He's rich and

spoiled. He's had many women. He may grow tired of you in time. If his oldest wife dies, perhaps he'll take another wife and you'll be used up."

"He has been kind to us . . ."

"Bah!" she says in a hoarse bellow. "Murad would have learned to love you for your intelligence and hard work."

"Murad is a good man," I say, trying to keep the sadness from my voice. "He will grow to love Phulan."

"Perhaps," says Sharma, stroking her chin.

"One thing you haven't thought of," says Fatima. "That Rahim-*sahib* chose Shabanu and not Phulan speaks well of him."

Sharma laughs heartily. "True!" she says, but her voice turns weary. "You girls know nothing of men. What he sees as spirit and intelligence now may look like insolence and trouble later."

She sits back against her bolster for the first time and lights a cigarette.

"Unless . . ." Fatima and I look at each other, and Fatima is smiling slightly. I wait as long as I can.

"Unless what?"

"Lower your voice, Shabanu," says Sharma. She takes my face in her hands and turns it from side to side. "You have a strong chin . . . your father's large gray eyes . . . your mother's straight nose . . ." She grabs the end of the braid that hangs over my shoulder and unties the goat-hair cord at its end.

"When was the last time you brushed your hair?" She turns me with my back to her and takes a brush in her hand. With long, merciless strokes, she untangles the hair that has grown matted from riding in the wind and walking in the rain, jerking my head back and silencing me when I cry out. Fatima sits giggling on the bed across from me.

"You know, there is a choice," Sharma says, yanking at my head. I spin around.

"What do you mean?'

"Sshh! Do you want to wake the whole desert? If your father hears, there won't be any choice."

She finishes brushing and stands me up, arranging the hair around my shoulders like a cape, the way Phulan has been wearing hers.

"It softens your chin," she says, tilting my face away to examine my profile. Then she pushes my hair back behind my shoulders. "You have lovely hair, long and wavy. It's better then Phulan's!" I flush with pleasure.

"What choice do I have, Auntie Sharma?" I whisper.

She rummages in a sack and hauls out a tin of dried and caked black eye makeup that looks as if it hasn't seen the light of day for years. She dips a tiny three-haired brush in a cup of water and squints with concentration as she outlines my eyes. Again she holds my chin, turning my face up to the golden glow of the kerosene lamp. She puts rouge on my lips. It tastes like soap. A smile spreads across her face slowly, lighting her up like the night when the stars come out.

"You do have a choice, my little quail," she says softly.

She stands me up again and pushes my shoulders back.

"What!" I demand in as soft a whisper as I can manage.

"You listen well at the *mahendi*," she says. The *mahendi* is the first ceremony of the wedding, when the women have their hands and feet painted with henna. They sit through the night singing and talking. The married women tell the bride the secrets of making a man happy. My eyes widen.

"Shabanu," says Sharma, "Fatima is right. There is a chance that you can keep Rahim-*sahib*'s interest if you learn some of the tricks of women."

"You said there was a choice," I say calmly, for my heart is thrashing inside my breast, and my mind is a confused jumble of fear, rebellion, pleasure, and curiosity.

"The choice is, you try to make him so happy he can't bear to be away from you a single moment. If he treats you badly, come stay with us."

She says it so simply I hardly believe the words.

"But Dadi would kill me—and you—all three of us!"

"Oh, he'd be angry," says Sharma. "But he'd never harm a hair on your head. And he wouldn't lay a hand on me!"

The Wedding

Eight days before the wedding our relatives pour in from the far reaches of Cholistan, a stream of people in desert pink, electric blue, and printed patterns. Their bright turbans and *chadr*s bob like boats on the monsoon mirage. Many walk, urging along herds of sheep, goats, and cows with whistles and shouts. Others ride camels in mirrored and tasseled wedding livery.

They shout greetings to one another, their voices mingling with the laughter of children and the creaking of ox and camel carts as they pull in from the desert.

Uncle arrives from Rahimyar Khan by jeep, and the relatives grow quiet when they hear the motor whine through loose sand in the distance. Uncle climbs down from the hired vehicle, brushing dust from his western trousers and lace-up shoes. His shirt bulges open between the buttons over his belly. His sons greet him with shouts and up-stretched arms, clinging to his jacket. He lifts them and they cover his face with kisses.

He pinches their cheeks and they squeal. Dadi and Uncle embrace and hold each other at arm's length, laughing and exchanging bits of news. Uncle looks over Dadi's head, eying our new gold jewelry.

"You did well at Sibi!" says Uncle.

"Much has happened since we last met," Dadi says. Uncle asks about Hamir's death, and they move away to talk alone. Uncle glances at me as Dadi tells him of my betrothal to Rahim-*sahib*.

Auntie is in the courtyard, clucking and fussing, happy to have Uncle with her again. His eyes follow her slimmer figure as she carries his clothes and bedding from the jeep.

Phulan nudges me and covers a smile with her *chadr*. Mama looks at her sharply, and I pull her away to say hello to Adil, who has arrived by camel with his wife, and the new infant—a son! Everyone makes a fuss over the baby boy: "He looks like Adil" and "His cheeks are so round . . ."

Adil's wife, a thin girl of sixteen, says little but smiles

at the compliments to her infant son. The little girls cling to her skirt.

Hundreds of cousins from both sides of the clan come with bundles of gifts. More lean-tos spring up along the edge of the desert as our relatives settle down for the celebration.

The monsoon sky is pearly with white, humid heat. There are showers in the afternoon, just enough to cool the air. Then the sun comes out, and vapor rises in curls and wisps.

"How lucky that Phulan's wedding is blessed with fair weather," says Mama as we sit in the courtyard in front of the houses, stitching last-minute gifts for Murad's family. Her eyes are bright. My thoughts turn to our *toba*, and I hope that the rain will fill it so we can return to Cholistan after the wedding.

Phulan spends her time sighing and lounging, pulling me aside to complain about a detail or to tell me how lucky she is or how unhappy she is.

"I'm so frightened, Shabanu," she says. "When things are so perfect I'm afraid something will go wrong again."

"You've had your bad luck," I tell her. "Now, stop talking that way."

I find her happiness painful, but I talk gently to her, glad when another group of relatives comes to leave gifts and admire her.

The musicians drift in amid the crowds of cousins and their animals—dozens of singers and drummers and *shenai* players, dancing to their own music and talking and laughing as they come. They play in the evenings around campfires in the desert and at the farm. Some of their music is haunting, some is joyous.

Sometimes, as I lie under the quilt looking up at the starlit sky, a lone shepherd beckons his sheep with a flute from the top of a distant dune. The music makes me long for Cholistan.

Rahim-*sahib* sends his man on the white horse again, this time with strands of pearls and rubies for Phulan to wear in her hair for the wedding.

"Oh, Shabanu," she whispers, her breath perfumed with fennel, "your future husband is wonderful!'

"He's used to buying what he wants," I say. Phulan's eyes widen and her lips part. "I wonder if he casts off what he buys after he doesn't want it."

"Shabanu!" she says, shocked.

"A man who takes four wives—even though the Koran allows it—must be greedy!"

"How can you say that?"

I clamp my mouth shut, but I am not ashamed of what I think. I decide not to say more for fear Phulan will tell Dadi.

In a clearing between our mud houses and the farm, a man with a stick stands guard, occasionally chasing off a swarm of children who descend upon men making sweets in heavy cauldrons surrounded by pungent smells and clouds of flies.

The men sing and dance late every night. The few times our own camp is quiet, raucous laughter and the throbbing of drums carry from the fields near Murad's house across the canal.

Two days before the wedding, Bibi Lal abandons her vigil over Hamir's grave at midday. In the golden evening light she heads a procession of women to our house for the *mahendi* celebration. Wearing a dress of muslin, the cloth of mourning, Bibi Lal looks like a giant white lily among her cousins and nieces, who carry baskets of sweets atop their flower-colored *chadr*s. They sing and dance through the fields, across the canal, to our settlement at the edge of the desert.

Sakina carries a wooden box containing henna. The *mahendi* women, Hindus from a village deep in the desert who will paint our hands and feet, walk behind her. Musicians and a happy cacophony of horns, pipes, and cymbals drift around them.

Mama, the servant girl, and I have prepared a curry of chicken, dishes of spiced vegetables, sweet rice, and several kinds of bread to add to the food that the women of Murad's family bring. We have brewed tea with cardamom and cinnamon in a huge cauldron that will remain on the fire through the night.

Sharma has washed and brushed my hair. I wear a new pink tunic. She lines my eyes and rubs the brilliant lapis powder into my lids. Fatima stains my lips and cheeks with the palest rouge. Sharma holds me away from her and turns me in a slow circle while they inspect me.

"You are lovely, my pigeon," says Sharma. "If you hold

your head high, you will tweak the hearts of any who think you are sad about losing Murad." Her wisdom is great enough to see the gaping black hole in my heart. I trust her more than any living soul. To please her I throw my shoulders back before I duck through the doorway.

Mama and Phulan follow me with their eyes when I emerge from Sharma's house, but Mama smiles, her look one of admiration and surprise more than disapproval.

We greet the women from Murad's family with warm embraces.

"You look beautiful. . . . Is this little Shabanu? She's grown into a woman!" Many of Murad's cousins are ours as well.

"Come, sit here, close to us."

They sit and talk with us until the sun sets. Then Bibi Lal leads them back to their settlement, leaving Phulan to a last night with the women of her family.

Our own close relatives settle in rings around the court-yard, Mama's closest cousins in front. They light fires and candles, and their laughter and talk enfold us.

The *mahendi* women open the carved wooden box and mix the musty-smelling clay with water. They pour the thick, reddish liquid into little ceramic bowls.

Phulan sits on a small stool in the center of the women. Her yellow *chadr* surrounds her in a golden glow. She wears no makeup and her skin is delicate and translucent, her lips pale. Her only jewelry is a tinkly silver chain around each ankle.

Mama is the first of seven married women to dip a finger into the bowl of henna and make a reddish dot on Phulan's outstretched palm.

I am ashamed of my anger that it is Phulan and not me sitting amid our relatives accepting advice on marrying Murad. But I mustn't feel sorry for myself. I press my shoulder blades together and lift my head.

We serve food and tea as a *mahendi* woman paints a delicate design around the seven marks on Phulan's palm.

It will be different when Rahim-*sahib* and I marry. His people will scorn us and our shoes with turned-up toes and rough cotton tunics. How I envy Phulan the warm circle of our women for the rest of her life!

The *mahendi* woman dips her slender index finger into the cup of red clay repeatedly, holding Phulan's palm flat. She bends her head in concentration on the intricate leaves and flowers of the tree of life, her finger deft and sure.

"Tell me, Sharma," Phulan says softly. "What am I supposed to learn tonight?"

Sharma sits beside Phulan, leaning against the bolster next to her and looking into her eyes. I move close to them.

"Do you know about love between a man and a woman?" Sharma asks. Phulan's cheeks darken, and she fixes her eyes downward on the Mogul pattern emerging on her palm.

"You must learn to please him," Sharma continues. Auntie is straining to hear, but Fatima, Mama, and I have taken the spots around Sharma and Phulan. The singing of the women has grown full and rhythmic, the beat marked by their clapping palms, the slapping of bare feet on the desert floor, and the jangle of ankle bells and bangles.

"I'll please him by having sons," says Phulan. "Isn't that what pleases a man most?"

"Bah!" says Sharma. "Having babies only stretches what will please him most."

Phulan gasps and Auntie puts her hand to her mouth. Fatima and I laugh, but Phulan is flustered, and Auntie moves away, her eyes scanning the closest circles for somewhere else to sit.

Sharma takes Phulan's face between her palms and looks into her eyes, speaking solemnly.

"Phulan, your beauty is great. But beauty holds only part of a man, and that for just so long. Keep some of yourself hidden. You can lavish love and praise on him and work hard by his side. Yes, and have your sons. That will help. But the secret is keeping your innermost beauty, the secrets of your soul, locked in your heart so that he must always reach out to you for it."

Phulan looks confused, but she smiles sweetly and thanks Sharma for the advice. Sharma's words lift my heart, and it soars like a partridge taking flight from the desert floor. I see myself in a new light, with value I'd never attached to myself before. There are secrets that will lie deep in my heart, for me alone. I repeat Sharma's exact words, committing them to memory, and know they are the perfect gift of wisdom.

Sharma, Mama, and I make room for other women who come to offer advice, and Phulan listens languidly to talk of putting magical herbs under Murad's pillow at night to stir his desire for her, and how she must look down when he speaks to her.

"I'm afraid your words were lost on her," Mama says to Sharma. "But she's beautiful, and I hope Murad will love her well enough. Perhaps he can teach her wisdom of his own."

Mama's words stab at my heart. I repeat Sharma's words, trying to apply them like medicine to a wound. Tears come to the back of my eyes, where I manage to hold them, but the pressure is painful. I swallow several times, and Fatima slips her hand over mine without looking at me.

I sit quietly while the *mahendi* women paint my own hands and feet. I am soothed by their quiet, steady hands, and by the voices of the singing and laughing women around me. I awake around dawn, without having been aware of falling asleep. The women fold their quilts, yawning, while a lone flute plays. Mama hands me a cup of spiced tea and sits down beside me, the fire crackling behind her. She looks tired.

"It will be time to dress Phulan soon," she says. I'd as soon dump the henna left standing in ceramic bowls over Phulan as dress her in jewels and silk to marry Murad.

"I know it's difficult, Shabanu," Mama says. "But you are young, and there is time for your heart to heal." She strokes my hair. "Sharma is right. In your way you are as great a beauty as your sister. But you have much to learn before your strength works *for* you instead of *against* you."

I throw my arms around her neck and hold her tight. The tears spill over. If I can be as wise and beautiful as she and Sharma, surely I'll be happy.

After checking that the kabob and sweets makers are ready for the feast, we pack the camels Dadi has given Phulan for her dowry with things for the house where she and Murad will live: a stone wheat grinder, goatskin water buckets, clay pots, butter churns, a string bed with carved wooden legs, clothes, reed mats, goathair carpets with saffron-dyed cords, woven bags for spices and rice. We leave the camels waiting in the shade of a canopy, their bells jingling.

I leave my cousins bustling in and out of the house carrying last-minute gifts, and go to the clearing behind the houses, where the rest of our camels eat from bags of fodder.

Mithoo gambols over to me, his head stretched out for a treat. I hold out a *jelabi.* He curls his lip at the syrupy twist of dough, then snatches it from the flat of my palm before dashing away. It's been several days since I've visited him.

I sit on the ground, my pink silk dress a brilliant circle around me. Mithoo comes up quietly behind me and plucks at my hair.

There is nothing I can do about losing Murad, just as there was nothing I could do about losing Guluband. Then without bidding, as I sit stroking Mithoo's neck, my heart releases Murad. For the first time I feel free—free to be happy for my sister, free to think about my future without him.

From the farm the large bronze drums beat, signaling that a camel race is about to start. Dadi and Uncle have been there with my boy cousins all morning, watching the dancing camels. The quavering melody of a *shenai* wafts across the desert on a breeze, and for the first time since Hamir's death I am at peace.

"There you are!" says Mama. "They'll be here soon."

"I'm ready." I get up, brushing the sand from my skirt, and follow her into the house.

Phulan sits squirming as Sharma brushes her hair. Her skin glistens from oil and sandalwood paste.

"Sit still!" says Sharma.

Mama lifts the *chadr* from Bibi Lal out of its box and unfolds the heavy red silk with butterflies and flowers embroidered in gold and green thread, the stitches so tiny they're barely visible. Phulan touches it delicately, as if it will crumble under her fingers.

Sharma pins Phulan's thick hair up, twisting the strings of rubies and pearls from Rahim-*sahib* into the strands around her face.

"You're hurting me!" Phulan says, a quaver in her voice. When Sharma is finished, Phulan is near tears.

The effect is a tremulous beauty that I am certain will seize Murad's heart the second he sees her. The *chadr* is the last thing to be put on, and Mama adjusts it so that it extends well over Phulan's face, hiding her in a demure cocoon.

Outside, the singing, dancing, jostling procession from Murad's house crosses the canal. The line snakes toward us slowly to the beat of drums and pipes and *shenai.*

Dust from the feet of hundreds of people in the procession seeps through the reed door. When we hear the music just outside, Dadi pokes his head in and looks at us.

"Your groom is here," he says to Phulan. "God go with you." It would be unlike Dadi to offer a compliment, but his eyes shine as he stands a second longer, looking at Mama, Phulan, and me before letting the door fall back into place.

Phulan is the last to emerge, Mama and I leading her by the hands. Her shoulders tremble under the red *chadr,* and I remember the nights under the quilt, when she cried in fear.

We deliver Phulan to Murad, who stands waiting with garlands of flowers, rupee notes, and gold threads around his neck.

A *maulvi* chants the call of the faithful in a high, nasal wail, and their vows are exchanged three times, with Phulan nodding her assent. Her face is hidden by the red *chadr;* her head is bowed, barely at the level of Murad's chin. She looks frail beside him.

When the ceremony is finished, Mama and Dadi pass baskets of dried dates among the guests, and the marriage is solemnized.

Mama and I lead Phulan to a platform with mirrored and embroidered bolsters scattered over red carpets. Garlands of roses and jasmine form a canopy overhead. Murad sits beside her. They do not touch or look at each other. They seem oblivious of the singing and dancing around the platform. Bibi Lal hands him a glass of sweetened milk. Murad drinks from it and hands it to Phulan. She dips her head and drinks, her first act of obedience to her husband. Bibi Lal holds a silver mirror under the red and gold *chadr* that hides Phulan's face. She and Murad peer shyly into the mirror, and their first glimpse of each other as man and wife is a reflected image.

When it's time for them to leave, Bibi Lal pulls the veil back from Phulan's face. She continues to stare down while Mama and I lead her to the camel where Murad waits to take her to her new home.

Our aunts hold the Koran overhead between them, making an arch through which Phulan passes. The women wail their sadness at Phulan's leaving. Mama's face is streaked with tears as she and I lead her to the waiting camel. Phulan's eyes are steady on the ground before her. Her shoulders stoop under the weight of the heavily embroidered silk, but her fingers are firm as she holds Mama and me by the hands until the very last second.

The huge, white silk turban on Murad's head reminds me briefly of the boy with the skinny neck and big ears. But now he wears a handsome mustache, and he holds out his hands to take Phulan's from Mama and me. He helps her onto the camel and climbs up in front of her.

222

The huge beast lurches to his feet, and my sister leaves her old life behind.

Mama, Sharma, Fatima, and I walk silently back to our house, our arms around each other's waists, all of us crying. The musicians leave with the procession, Murad's male cousins dancing and singing, their voices hoarse.

The next day at the feast given by Murad's family, Rahim-*sahib* waits with the other guests. My heart lurches when I see him, his eyes fastened on me as I walk with Mama and Dadi. He wears an elaborate striped turban. My shoulders are straight and my head is high. I meet his gaze for a moment, then turn my head to look for Phulan. I feel Rahim-*sahib*'s eyes on the side of my face, half hidden in the shadow of my *chadr,* and they follow me through the afternoon. I don't look at him again, but my face burns, half in pleasure, half in discomfort. My belly tightens and my mouth is dry.

Cholistan

As soon as the wedding is over, our relatives return to the desert much as they arrived, in a symphony of animal bells.

Sharma and Fatima are among the last to leave. I visit them where they gather their sheep and goats amid bleating and thumping hooves from the scrub bushes at the edge of the desert. We sit under a thorn tree, and Sharma holds me close to her.

"Oh, Sharma, I would have been lost if you hadn't been here!"

"Remember when the time comes that you have a choice, pigeon," she says. I shake my head against her shoulder. "Don't make any silly mistakes now. You have important decisions ahead of you."

I lie against her for some time, taking comfort from her large brown hand stroking my hair and the earthy, desert smell of her.

"But there isn't any choice! I must marry him, or his brother will ruin Phulan's life." I pluck at her skirt, my fingers pleating and unpleating the soft, worn fabric. "Even if I'm desperately unhappy, I can never leave him."

Sharma looks at me steadily, her fingers firm on my shoulders. The shade of the tree dapples over us, softening the deep lines on her forehead.

"No matter what happens, you have *you*. That is the important thing. And as long as you have you, there is always a choice." I can't answer.

"I watched Rahim-*sahib* during the wedding," she says. "His eyes never left you. They begged you to look at him. And when you did, his face softened. He's in love with you, Shabanu. He'll want you to be happy."

"But don't you see? If Rahim-*sahib* loves me, it will be even worse. His other wives despise me already because I'm a desert girl. If he loves me, they will make life unbearable!"

Sharma nods and is quiet for a moment.

225

"You will have to be very wise and guard his affection closely."

"But once I've started to have babies, by the time I'm sixteen I'll look like Adil's wife or Kulsum. He'll start looking for another woman younger than me to fall in love with."

A secret smile steals over Sharma's face, and she leans back against the tree trunk.

"You don't have to look like Adil's wife or Kulsum. He already has sons. He doesn't need children from you. But you'll need a child of your own for him to adore. There are ways of keeping your body strong and healthy through childbearing. You will be beautiful long after Phulan is old."

"How?"

"I'll tell you when the time is right," she says. "You have enough to worry about now."

"I want to know! I've watched babies being born and people die . . ."

"Soon enough, child," she says. "But remember: you will always have a place with Fatima and me near Fort Abbas if you want to come."

"Oh, Sharma, should I come? Tell me what you think!"

"I can offer you help, regardless of what decision you make. But you are the only one who can decide."

"We must make a plan!" I say, panicking at the thought of Sharma leaving.

"That is for you alone to do," she says. "Keep your

wits about you. Trust yourself. Keep your inner reserves hidden. You know where to find me if you need me."

My panic rises again as Mama, Dadi, and I say good-bye to Sharma and Fatima, and I stand looking after them long after her herd has disappeared among the dunes.

There is danger along both paths I might take, and I am confused and unsure of myself without her.

Our return to Cholistan fills me with a double-sided happiness, my joy in the desert the dearer because I dread what lies ahead.

Dadi tries to cheer me by singing the rhymes we'd sung on our way to Sibi. I join him, with Mama and my cousins clapping the rhythm. Xhush Dil lifts his legs in an elegant, musical walk. At almost the same moment, Mithoo's feet kick out in a clumsy, adolescent dance. Dadi's head whips around at the sound of the small camel leg bells behind him, and he loses his balance. He falls from his seat in front of Xhush Dil's hump, landing on his backside in a bush beside the trail.

Mama laughs until tears spill as he struggles to free his *lungi* from the bush and then to catch up with the dancing camels. I laugh, and the tightness in my throat relaxes.

I hear Sharma's voice saying "Fold your happiness deep in your heart," and I tuck this moment away in my reserve of happy memories.

No matter how hard Dadi shouts for Xhush Dil to stop, the great beast senses the joke and dances faster, kicking his feet higher, his ears pitched forward, his head turning from side to side for his audience to admire. Even Auntie and Uncle whoop with laughter, and the boys collapse against each other.

"When did you teach Mithoo to dance?" Dadi asks, his breath coming in great gulps as he regains his seat on Xhush Dil's back.

"I guess it came naturally to him," I say, smiling.

I know Mama and Dadi miss Phulan, and their efforts to be cheerful make me feel close to them.

Just as the weather had cleared for the wedding, it begins to rain again as we near the *toba*. Returning home during rain is a good omen, and everyone is in high spirits as we ride into our little settlement.

Much of the sand from the storm that sent us fleeing to Derawar has blown away, and the area looks more familiar than it did when we left it.

Mama, Auntie, and I rush to unload the camels before our belongings get soaked, and Dadi goes off to see if the wind has blown the *toba* clear of sand and whether it will hold water.

We unload the reed mats first, and Uncle climbs onto the roof to secure them over the holes torn by the storm. Auntie, Mama, and I pull our bedding inside the huts. I set out a row of empty jars to catch the rain, which falls in great, sweet *plips* against the red clay.

I make a fire, and the smoke rises and twists in a fine strand to escape through the thatch. My heart gives a small lurch of happiness.

The house seems both smaller and larger. We've grown used to being able to stand up straight in the mud house Rahim-*sahib* built, and yet without Phulan, Grandfather, and the dowry trunk, there is more room than before.

Tea is ready by the time Dadi comes in.

"The *toba* has blown nearly clean," he says, peeling off his tunic. "We can clear out the remaining sand in a day or two. If this rain keeps up, we'll have more water than last year."

"Next year we'll be hoping for enough water to stay until it's time to leave for your wedding," Mama says, looking at me.

I don't answer, and Dadi pokes at the fire.

"If Phulan has a baby before then, can I go to her?" I ask. Dadi and Mama look at each other, the firelight dancing across their faces.

"She is part of Murad's family now," says Mama.

"But if Bibi Lal were to ask us?"

"We'll see," says Dadi. "It's a long time from now, and we have your wedding to plan."

I sigh and pull a camel harness in need of repair into my lap.

The next morning the air is cool and clear for summer because of the rain. I fold my quilt, and just as I duck out the door Dadi calls me back.

"Where are you going?" His voice is stern.

I'm not sure how to answer. Every morning of my life in the desert I've been the first one up and out to see the camels.

"You stay here and help your mother prepare breakfast," he says. I step back inside, staring at him.

"But—"

"It's time your cousins begin to look after the camels. And it's long past time you learned how to look after a house."

"They aren't old enough to—"

"Shh, shh," says Mama. "Come here, Shabanu." As I go to her, Dadi gets up in a single, fluid motion and walks outside.

"I know how to make breakfast and look after the house," I say, my voice shaking with indignation. "Why can't I do it after I've looked at the camels? I haven't seen the *toba* yet and—"

"Shabanu, your father is trying to tell you that your responsibility now is to learn how to run a house. Remember when Phulan was betrothed and she had to stay at home? Now it is your time."

I shake my head, ready to argue again. But Sharma's words come back to me: "Don't make any silly mistakes now."

I spend the morning sweeping the courtyard and mixing clay, cow dung, and water to repair the mud walls that have begun to crumble in the monsoon rains. Uncle and Dadi go out to collect branches of *khip* to repair the thatch roofs, leaving the boys standing with the camels and leaning importantly on long sticks.

I don't even have the excuse of going out for water,

and Auntie has collected milk from the camels. The day is as gray as my mood, and it seems to stretch on forever.

In the afternoon, on the pretext of looking for mushrooms, I wander toward the *toba*. Hearing the jangle of my ankle bracelets, Mithoo comes trotting out from somewhere deep in the herd. He sticks his nose under my arm, and I produce a lump of brown sugar for him.

I'm so happy to see him that I throw my arms around his neck and bury my face in his fur. I wonder if this is all the happiness there will be for the rest of my life: stealing a few moments from a day of housework to sit quietly in the desert with my camels. I wonder how I will endure.

Again I hear Sharma's words: "Keep your inner reserves hidden." And I try to appreciate the joy of the moment without the sorrow.

The days pass slowly, thoughts of what my life will be like tumbling over and over inside my head. I try to concentrate on my choices.

If I marry Rahim-*sahib,* there will be servants. I won't have to do housework, but my life will belong to him. If he wants me to be happy, he will leave me alone to be in the desert with the animals.

But that's impossible for a married woman. And even if it were not, it wouldn't be the same without my freedom.

Perhaps I could learn to read and write. Would he be afraid of a woman who can do such things? Perhaps I could learn to play the flute. . . .

If I go to live with Sharma I will be free. But if freedom comes at the cost of my sister's well-being, how sweet will it be?

When I go now to the *toba* to bathe, I inspect my fast-growing breasts half with pleasure, half with fear. They are already full and round, and I hope they will be like Fatima's. But the rapid rate of growth means my coming of age is near. I try to keep it away by sheer will. I hope vaguely that I am defective, that the monthly bleeding will never begin, that Rahim-*sahib* will not want me after all.

We work hard building new underground mud tanks with caps that will keep the water from disappearing into the air when the hot weather returns next spring. The thought of being able to stay in the desert until my wedding is arranged gives me some comfort.

Dadi and Uncle dig, and Mama and I mix clay, sand, and water. They plaster the surface that has been dug and let it dry before digging deeper and repeating the process until we have six perfect underground water jugs.

A late monsoon storm cooperates by pouring rain into the cisterns. When they're full, we seal them. They will remain sealed until the *toba* is dry next spring.

The rains stay another month, and the air turns cooler. One day when I go out into the desert to relieve myself in the opal haze of an autumn morning, I notice a rusty stain on my inner thigh, and panic steals into my heart.

"Keep your wits about you," I hear Sharma say.

That evening I search through the goathair bag in which Mama keeps the clothes Phulan and I have worn out, and

I tear an old skirt into strips. I can't tell them, not yet. I need more time.

Another month passes, and I manage to bury the cloths from the second bleeding in the desert, so Mama doesn't find out. I am so lonely and afraid I want to die. Why couldn't I have an empty head like Phulan, with thoughts of sons and new dresses enough to make me happy?

Every night I curl up under the quilt pretending to sleep. But sleep eludes me. I burn with shame when I hear Mama and Dadi making love. The thought of Rahim-*sahib* in my bed, his hands on my body, frightens me, perhaps the more so because I also have begun to feel desire.

I touch myself in the night and wonder how it would feel to have a man touch me.

One night as I huddle under the quilt, Mama and Dadi sit talking in the yellow glow of the kerosene lamp while Mama folds the clothes she has washed that day.

"I think it's time we contact Rahim-*sahib* to set a date for Shabanu's wedding," says Mama.

"Why?" asks Dadi. "Has she come of age?"

"I'm almost certain, though she hasn't told me. I went to the cloth bag today to make a new plug for the water trough, and it was nearly empty."

My heart thunders, the blood roaring in my ears. Dadi is silent for a moment.

"What does she mean by keeping secrets?" he says, his voice shaking with anger.

"Shh, shh," says Mama.

"I'll throttle her!"

"What will that accomplish?" asks Mama, her voice an urgent whisper. "She doesn't want to marry Rahim-*sahib*. Give her time to come to terms . . ."

"It isn't a matter of what she wants!" He speaks in a harsh whisper.

"She is a sensitive child," says Mama.

"She is not a child, she's a woman!" he says.

"She is intelligent and—"

"She'll find out where her intelligence will get her," says Dadi, the anger like ice in his voice.

There is no question of my going to sleep, and I make up my mind. I will not be beaten. I will not marry a man whose wives will make me their slave. I'll die first.

It will take a full twenty-four hours to reach Sharma at Fort Abbas. I will take Xhush Dil.

When Mama and Dadi finally sleep, I reach down and remove my ankle bracelets so I can move without noise. My leg has grown, and the silver cuffs are tight and difficult to take off. Dadi stirs in his sleep as one of them rattles. I wait a minute, barely breathing, then slip silently out from under the quilt. I undress and arrange the bedding so they won't know I'm gone if they wake.

I find the pile of clothes Mama folded before she went to bed, and remove one of Dadi's *lungi*s, a turban, an undershirt, and a tunic.

I slip out into the courtyard without making a sound. By the filmy light of a sliver of moon and stars muted by clouds, I pull the undershirt over my head and hold it tight as I wind the *lungi* around my waist. My breasts flatten against my chest, and the tunic is big enough over it that my breasts are hidden. I pull my hair up and tie it in a knot, then twist the turban around my head.

I hope I'll be mistaken for a boy, with my broad face and short, wide hands and feet.

In the corner of the courtyard a wooden saddle stands on its end. I hoist it to my shoulder and stop dead in my tracks as Sher Dil comes out of Auntie's house, stretching and yawning. I pray he won't bark at me, but he just sniffs at my feet and looks at me expectantly. I let him follow me to the *toba,* where Xhush Dil and the other camels stand near the water.

Mithoo trots up to me and I slip a piece of brown sugar onto his tongue before he starts to grunt and snort, and I wonder whether I'll be able to get away without Mithoo and Sher Dil following. I have a piece of sugar for Xhush Dil, too. He chews it while I remove his ankle bracelets.

"Uushshshsh," I whisper, and Xhush Dil grunts softly as he folds his front legs under him, lowering himself gracefully to the ground. When the saddle is in place, I fill a jar with water and secure it with a goathair cord before climbing onto his back.

I marvel at how calm I am, and as Xhush Dil rises to his feet a rush of hope fills my heart.

I turn Xhush Dil toward the dunes, and with time to put a large piece of desert between me and my sleeping father before sunrise, I feel safe, as if nothing can harm us. Mithoo follows us, and I try to shoo him away. Sher Dil turns back toward the *toba,* where he sits, his tail curled around his feet, watching, as if wishing me luck. But Mithoo will not go away.

I get down from the saddle and lead Mithoo to the thorn tree where we sat the day he was born. He follows me eagerly, kicking up his feet to please me. I tie him to the tree, but he begins to struggle and complain. I quickly untie him again before he wakes everyone, and he nuzzles me gratefully. I put my arms around his neck and bury my face in his fur. I couldn't leave him for all the world.

"You'd better be quick, then," I tell him, removing his ankle bracelets too. He follows me back to Xhush Dil, ducking his head and skipping as I climb up onto the large camel. Mithoo trots beside us, up and over the first row of dunes.

Although the dunes take longer than following the hard-packed track, I keep to them in the hope that the breeze will gather force and blow enough sand to cover the camels' footprints.

I'm certain Dadi will follow us along the track, but if he doesn't, I don't want him to know how we've gone. I try to keep the North Star on my shoulder, but it's difficult because of the clouds. Perhaps if I'm lucky it will rain, and our tracks will disappear altogether.

But the clouds clear and the wind dies, and I curse the sapphire sky I love for fear it will give me away.

I keep waiting for the enormity of my flight to frighten me or to make me sorry—knowing that I'm letting Mama and Dadi down, that Murad could lose his farm, that I could be caught and beaten.

But nobody felt sorry or frightened for me when they offered me to Rahim-*sahib*. No one even asked how I felt.

My only worry is that Sharma will think I've acted stupidly. But it's done, and I'll know what she thinks soon enough.

And if Rahim-*sahib* tries to find me, I will hide from him the rest of my life. If he is such a decent man, perhaps he will let me go without letting his brother punish my family.

Mithoo keeps up without difficulty, although I keep Xhush Dil moving at a fast pace. The air is soft and moist against my face, and the camels' feet whisper softly through the loose sand.

The stars fade as dawn nears. When Dadi wakes at sunup he will find us gone. When he follows, the distance of half a night's travel will be between us.

I think of the Bugti girl in Baluchistan, and suddenly her bravery is not such a mystery. She did what she did of necessity. Perhaps, like me, she had only one chance for happiness.

Mithoo begins to tire, but I urge him on. He's still very young, his energy going into his growth. If I'd tied him to the thorn tree he would have bellowed until all of Cholistan was awake. Even if his slower pace costs us an hour, it will be impossible for Dadi to catch up with us. And I am happy to have him with me.

The farther I go, the more fully I sense freedom, leaving my spirit fresh and light. I think of Sharma and Fatima and me, our animals and the clothes on our backs our only possessions, the desert our only worry.

Behind me I hear a thud and a grunt, then a frightened bleating. Xhush Dil slows of his own accord and turns back toward the sound. I can't see much, but the thrashing and frightened cries are easy to follow, growing in intensity with fear and pain. My heart expands to fill my entire chest, and my breath comes in thin, fast gasps.

I see a struggling form on the ground and leap down before Xhush Dil reaches a stop. I can't see immediately what has happened, but Mithoo struggles, unable to get to his feet. He stretches out his neck to me, his chin working. I try to quiet him with my hands, soothing him with my voice.

"Mithoo, Mithoo, you'll be all right. Let's just get you up and see what's happened . . . " Hope guides my fingers along his legs and then evaporates as they touch a warm, sticky mass of fur around a foreleg that is buried in the sand above the knee. He must have stepped into a foxhole.

In half a second I know the leg is broken.

He is still for a moment, quieted by his trust in me. But his breath is shallow with pain. I lean my forehead against his side. He cannot walk, and I cannot leave him. The jackals would get him before dawn.

So I pray. I pray that Dadi will find us soon and that we can get Mithoo back to the *toba* on Xhush Dil's back. Mithoo weighs twice what I weigh—there is no question of my being able to lift him myself. I pray that he'll survive, that his leg will mend. I pray that Dadi will forgive my one hope for freedom. I know he will beat me, but that doesn't matter. I know my fate is sealed.

"Oh, Mithoo, what have I done to you?" I cry softly and he nuzzles me. My heart shatters inside me. Mithoo will never dance again. I sob into his fur, and he rests his chin on my knee as I hold his neck in my arms.

I stretch out beside him, and both of us are calm, waiting for dawn. I am not afraid for myself. I feel like nothing else can ever hurt me again. Like Guluband, I have been betrayed and sold. And Mithoo, like me, has lost his greatest gift by wanting to follow his heart.

The sky clears as the palest pink outline appears over the tops of the dunes. I'm grateful it hasn't rained and wiped out our footprints. I want Dadi to find us quickly. Perhaps another hour, if he has been able to follow our tracks.

Lying on the ground, I feel the vibrations of a camel's feet pounding across the desert floor. The vibrations disappear as the camel rises up and over a dune. Then the pounding begins again. Xhush Dil and Mithoo turn their ears in the direction from which we've come.

Dadi's face shows no expression when he sees us, just as the sun rises. It's as if he'd expected us to be here in this exact spot all along.

Without speaking he lifts me to my feet and brings his stout stick down across my shoulders. I stand straight and let the stick fall against my ribs and shoulders. I am silent. "Keep your reserves hidden." I repeat Sharma's words over and over, drawing on the strength of my will.

I refuse to cry out, and Dadi in his fury is like Tipu, bloodlust in his eyes. He can beat me to death if he likes. The pain grows worse as the blows strike already-bruised flesh. But I take Sharma's advice. I recall the beautiful things in my world and, like a bride admiring her dowry, I take them out, one by one, then fold them away again, deep into my heart.

I hear sobbing, as if from a great distance, and my knees crumple. Dadi catches me in his arms and buries his face against my bloody tunic. He holds me against him, and through a haze of pain, I realize it is Dadi sobbing, not me.

"The secret is keeping your innermost beauty, the secrets of your soul, locked in your heart," Sharma's voice whispers in my ear, "so that he must always reach out to you for it."

Rahim-*sahib* will reach out to me for the rest of his life and never unlock the secrets of my heart.

Glossary

Allah (*Ah*-luh)—God in Arabic, the language of the Islamic
   religion.

Allah-o-Akbar (*Ah*-luh *oh Ahk*-bahr)—"God is great!"

Asalaam-o-Aleikum (Uh-suh-*lahm* oh Uh-*leh*-koom)—Traditional
   greeting.

betel (*beet*-uhl)—A nut with red juice and narcotic properties.

bhai (*bhii*)—Brother.

Bugti (*Buhg*-tee)—A tribe living in eastern Iran, southwestern
   Pakistan, and southern Afghanistan.

chadr (*chad*-duhr)—A cloth worn by women as a head cover.

chapati (chah-*pah*-tee)—A flat, round bread made of whole wheat
   and water and cooked in a flat pan over an open fire.

Eid (*Eed*)—An Islamic festival that ends a period of fasting.

ghazal (*ghuh*-zuhl)—A poem sung to drum and flute music.

Guluband (*Goo*-loo-buhnd)—The family's finest camel.

hookah (*hoohk*-uh)—A tall pipe with a small brass bowl in which
   tobacco and raw sugar are burned. The smoke is drawn through
   water held in the pipe base into a long, flexible mouthpiece.

hunteray (*huhnt*-uhr-eh)—"Giddyap!" to a camel.

Islam (*Ihs*-lahm)—A monotheistic religion of the Middle East,
   Africa, and Asia.

jelabi (juh-*leh*-bee)—A pretzel-shaped, deep-fried sweet.

jelabi-wallah (juh-*leh*-bee *wah*-luh)—*Jelabi*-maker.

kabob (kuh-*bahb*)—Cubes of meat roasted on a stick over a fire.

kafi (*kah*-fee)—A religious poem set to music.

Kalu (*Kah*-loo)—A young camel in the herd. His name means "black."

kharin (*khuh*-reen)—A green desert plant with edible sweet red flowers.

khip (*kihp*)—A brushy desert plant used to thatch roofs.

Koran (Kuh-*rahn*)—The holy book of Islam, written in the Arabic language.

krait (*kreht*)—A deadly snake.

lungi (*luhn*-gee)—A long piece of cloth usually worn wrapped around the waist.

mahendi (muh-*hehn*-dee)—Part of the marriage ceremony in which women have their hands and feet painted in intricate designs with henna.

Marri (*Muh*-ree)—A tribe of Baluchistan.

maulvi (*mohl*-vee)—An Islamic priest.

mehrab (muh-*rahb*)—Walls built to show Muslims in which direction they should bow to face Mecca for prayer.

Mithoo (Meet-*hoo*)—A baby camel whose name means "sweet."

mujahideen (muh-*jah*-hih-*deen*)—Muslim fighters engaged in battle with a non-Muslim enemy.

Muslim (*Muh*-slihm)—A person who follows the religion of Islam.

nawab (*nuh*-wahb)—A Muslim king of one of nearly 700 princely states that once formed part of what is now India and Pakistan.

paan (*pahn*)—A delicacy made of leaves and nuts of the betel plant plus other ingredients, such as fennel seed, sugar, and other spices.

pashmina (puhsh-*mee*-nah)—A fine wool used to make soft shawls.

Pathan (Puh-*tahn*)—A nation of tribal people who live mainly in Afghanistan and Pakistan's North-West Frontier Province.

pogh (*pohg*)—A thorny desert plant that camels like to eat.

Rajput (*Rahj*-puht)—A race of Hindu desert warriors in India.

Ramadan (*Rah*-muh-*dahn*)—The month of daytime fasting in the Islamic religion.

rupee (*roo*-pee)—The money of India and Pakistan. A Pakistani rupee is worth about six cents in United States money.

sahib (*suh*-hihb)—A respectful title.

salaam (suh-*lahm*)—A greeting.

shatoosh (*shah*-toosh)—A shawl made of wool so fine it can pass through a lady's ring.

shenai (shuh-*nii*)—An oboelike musical instrument.

Sher Dil (*Shurh* Dihl)—A puppy whose name means "lion heart."

sito (*see*-too)—A desert plant with a sweet, succulent root used as a source of water in a drought.

subadar (*suhb*-dahr)—Officer's rank in the Desert Rangers.

syed (*sii*-yiht)—An Islamic religious leader who traces his lineage back to the prophet Mohammed.

Tipu (*Tih*-poo)—A young male camel named for an eighteenth-century explorer.

toba (*toh*-buh)—A freshwater pond that serves as a water supply for desert nomads.

Xhush Dil (*Hoosh* Dihl)—A camel whose name means "happy heart."

SUZANNE FISHER STAPLES grew up in northeastern Pennsylvania and graduated from Cedar Crest College with a degree in literature and political science. She worked for many years as a UPI correspondent in Asia, including stints in Hong Kong, Pakistan, Afghanistan, and India, and later in Washington, D.C. She also worked on the foreign news desk of *The Washington Post*. During her years in Pakistan she became involved with the nomads of the Cholistan Desert. "It was the unfailing generosity and courage of the people of the Cholistan that inspired me to write this book," she says.

Staples lives with her writer husband in Bayford on the Chesapeake Bay's Eastern Shore. This is her first book.